BRANDED

A Tony Simons Series

Larry & Shirley Crandell

Publishers: McNally Robinson/Larry & Shirley

Crandell 2019

ISBN: 1-77280259X

Edited by: Kathryn Crandell and Garry & Brenda Boese

Cover Image By DiegoMariottini/Shutterstock.com

"Be yourself---everybody else is taken"

-Oscar Wilde

Prologue

Tony was walking to the train station with a determination that was new to him. It was a bright, sun shiny fall day and as he walked he could hear the crunch of leaves under his feet. Since his focus was getting to the train station, he paid no attention to the traffic or to the people walking past him.

Tony started to think about why he was here and what had brought him to this point in his life at 19 years old.

It was like snapshots of a bad movie playing over and over again in his head, fade in, fade out.

Blood all over him and not all his own, children screaming and women with terror-stricken looks in their eyes, fade out.

Six thugs bringing him to the ground to beat the hell out of him just because they wanted his cigarettes, fade out.

"You're Dick's kid aren't you?" Then he sees himself beating him to the ground with hate in his eyes, fade out.

"They call me Timber" fade out.

"Get on your bike and leave now!" as the bloody battle raged on all around him, fade out.

Racing his Harley down the QEW at 100mph with tears in his eyes, fade out.

Faces, faces, faces, fade out.

Tony bumped into an older lady; he had not been looking where he was going and it brought him back to reality. He apologized. She smiled and said it was ok and moved on.

He had been looking at his life to this moment. It was just a bad movie that was about to end. He felt the freedom in his hand as he gripped his travel orders tightly.

Chapter 1

Tony Simons' family history started in New England but his grandfather Ben moved to Port Nichols, Ontario looking for a new future.

Ben joined the Air Force, working as a mechanic and when the war ended he took odd jobs in engine shops and repaired broken farm machinery. His wife, Daisy, was Native born from Lewis port, New York. Ben met Daisy while working on a farm in the states one summer. They fell in love, married, and raised their family in and around Port Nichols. Eventually Ben found work on a large farm and the owner had a cottage where Ben and his family could live. It finally gave the family stability.

Ben's family consisted of six, including four children. After World War II it was normal to have large families because of a Government incentive called the "Baby Bonus." The more kids you had, the more money you received. With the war ended, this money was well-received by the working class; Ben and Daisy were normal working-class people.

Their children also grew up in the area and settled in and around Port Nichols. However, they did not have the drive that their parents had. It was like an entire arm of the Simons family tree had withered up and died.

Sarah, the youngest, was much like her mother but blind at birth. She married a young farmer that committed suicide soon after her giving birth to their one and only child, a boy. Fate was not yet finished with Sarah, for the child also died at a young age. She found it very hard to adapt after this sequence of events. Sometimes she would just sit in a corner with her hands folded on her lap, seemingly staring straight ahead. Defeated, Sarah eventually, quietly faded away with a man no one knew, never to be seen again.

Danny, the next oldest, tried to follow his father's proud military past and joined the Army. He fought in Korea and came home a beaten man. He was never the same and went insane dying alone in a mental hospital, a forgotten man.

Reggie, the third oldest proved to be more resourceful than his siblings. Along with having a house full of kids, he avoided work, claiming an injury to his back that no one could identify. He'd send his wife out to clean houses for money. He relied on Welfare and Baby Bonus money to get along.

He fancied himself a country and western singer. He would sing in bars and play his guitar at gatherings where he knew he could make money. His time in the bars led him to a life of heavy drinking and along with smoking brought him to an early death.

Dick, who was the oldest, was nasty and lazy. He never finished school. He was diagnosed with Diabetes at an early age and used it as an excuse to do nothing. He and his father never got along. Ben tried to instill a sense of pride in his children for hard work, self discipline and self worth. Dick rebelled against his father. He felt that his father worked way too hard for next to nothing. Dick didn't want this man, who he thought was a failure, to tell him what to do. Dick left school after grade six and Ben tried to get him to help on the farm where they lived but Dick liked sitting around way too much and as soon as he was 18 Ben told him he needed to go out into the world and find out how it really was. .

Dick thought he knew everything and to hell with his old man! He knew he needed money so he did find work for a while driving a dump truck, hauling asphalt. It didn't last long. Working with asphalt is a timely exercise. Dick wasn't the type to be rushed and he didn't like to be told what to do. He didn't deliver the asphalt on time and it hardened in the truck box and bent the box up in the middle. He found himself unemployed again.

Dick knew just what he was going to do next, he'd apply for Welfare! This began a roller coaster and a lifetime of working the system. When he was 21, Dick happened to be in a café. He felt a craving for a piece of pie and a cup of coffee. There he met Darlene. They hit it off right away. It turned out that they were both pretty much cut from the same cloth. They married in the courthouse soon after and settled in the Port Nichols area.

Port Nichols was founded in the 18th century. Most people looking around the pier in Port Nichols would see large two storey houses, situated on a bluff overlooking Lake Ontario. There were walkways along the canals where everything from sand dredgers to small sail boats would be docked. There was even an old lighthouse that still worked and added to the landscape. There were dock side restaurants and Folk Art Galleries located along wooden sidewalks where heritage houses were also established. The town's core was very scenic with brick buildings, parks, and in the summer time there would be bands playing and flea markets would be bustling.

This is what most people saw, but it was not the Port Nichols that Tony knew. Most of the town was broken up into ethnic areas; the projects being made up of predominately Christian German; the industrial downtown area was run by the Irish which was close to the factories; and the "Hill" which was a mishmash of a number of groups, but mainly claimed by the Italians. It was one of the worst areas in town. Tony spent most of his first 16 years moving around the projects, hand to mouth and trying to stay alive.

If you were ever introduced to the Simons family, initially you would think they were normal and hard working. Remember that looks can be deceiving. If you pulled back the veil of secrecy, you would see the real truth.

The Simons family consisted of his mom, Darlene; his father Dick; and two siblings; his older sister, Sybil and a younger brother, Ronnie.

His sister, Sybil was quiet by nature and didn't complain. She kept her head down and never looked anybody in the eye. However, she left home as soon as she could, married young, had children of her own and never looked back.

Tony's younger brother, Ronnie, was a skinny kid with dark blue eyes and had a big head covered with blond curly hair. When you looked at him you would think "sweet." He was anything but. He stuck around home for a time and was treated better. He could do no wrong and he knew it. He was the baby of the family and got away with murder. At every opportunity he made Tony's life a living hell. Whenever he got into trouble he would blame it on Tony and Tony would get a beating. He only finished grade six, took mainly to the streets after that and wound up in reform school.

Tony's family life was a train wreck. Tony's parents were little more than a joke to him. His mother was less than maternal. She had strawberry blond hair, she was tall, and never quite gave up her youth and all the behavior that went with it. She smoked and drank beer with her brother. She would take off for days at a time and end up with other men. She rarely worked, but she and her sister got jobs working at a car wash once, hand washing cars. This only lasted until they got one paycheck, which she quickly drank away. She was close to her sister who died way too young and Tony's mother never got over it. Needless to say with all her distractions it was not hard to understand that the boys were able to run amuck.

Darlene was always looking to escape, and since there was none, she drank. She was an ugly drunk, and mean. She would drink for days on end if she could get it, and got meaner and meaner until she would turn on the old man and blame him for their situation. She physically attacked him once, in one of her drinking binges. She grabbed him by the hair and tried to pull him to the floor. She seemed crazed. He punched her in the face and knocked her out. The old man was a coward.

There were times that Tony came home to a house that smelled of booze and cigarettes and there was no food in sight.

The prize of the household was Dick.

Chapter 2

Dick wasn't as tall as his wife and he had a stout build, he was as hairy as a gorilla and had a head of thick wavy dark brown hair that was his pride and joy. It was the only thing he seemed to have inherited from his father.

Dick made sure that Tony did not have an easy upbringing. He sent Tony to work at anything he could from the time Tony was 12. Tony then had to turn the money over to his father to "help the family" he'd say.

Dick had a friend who had a taxi and now and then he let Dick drive "off the meter." During one of these times, he picked up a sailor from the docks, who had just arrived for shore leave, and he had just got paid. Dick took him around to the bars and cat houses until he got really drunk. Then he took him back to the docks, knocked him out and rolled him. He then split approximately $2000 with his buddy who owned the taxi.

It was then time to take the family on vacation for the next four days because this was how long the sailor would be in town and Dick knew that he would be looking for him. Dick took the family camping! He used some of the money to buy a small camper trailer! Tony never saw him move so fast. He wanted the whole family packed up and in the car immediately! It turned out that it wasn't much of a holiday; it was more of a hideaway. Dick spent most of his time looking over his shoulder. Once back, he sold the trailer, it had served its purpose. Dick really preferred to live off "the system." Welfare was more his style.

Other than driving the taxi now and then Dick never worked. He always said "no one would hire me; I have diabetes!" He used this excuse to his advantage especially when he wanted to get something for nothing.

Dick liked to watch TV and tinker with his old car, not a classic, just a piece of shit car that he could afford. He fancied himself an auto mechanic, but everything he touched turned to shit. Nothing was ever Dick's fault; it was always someone else's. He played the victim card very well.

He destroyed the family name in town because he never worked a day in his life and he knew how to use the welfare system to his advantage. He was always "borrowing" money that he would never repay. He'd run up charges at some of the local stores and never repay. He often sent Tony to the

store with a note begging for food and cigarettes and saying
that he would pay later. This went to the very core of Tony's
character. Dick would go to the church and tell them how
hard things were and they'd wind up giving him food and
clothing chits. Dick also got food from a friend in the
neighbourhood that worked in the slaughter house. John
would bring him boxes of pig's feet and cow's hearts. Dick's
uncle, who lived on a reservation in the states, would bring
food in the form of blocks of cheese, tobacco and bear meat
to Dick's mother and she in turn would give his family
some.

Dick used to think he was tough, always flexing his
muscles. He would point his finger at Tony's face and say
"they nick named me Timber, because when I hit them, they
go down like fallen trees." The only people he could
intimidate were kids and Tony knew it. He was such a jerk.
Tony was ashamed of him.

Tony's parents were not positive role models the way
parents should be, so he seemed to be searching, always
searching. It was hard to be proud of himself, hard to be
proud of his name. Whenever anyone found out his name
was "Simons," they asked if he was Dick Simons' kid and
told him that his dad owed them money. He wasn't Tony
Simons, he was Dick Simons' kid and he was immediately
connected to his family's reputation, and the burden that

came with it. Tony felt dirty and it was hard for him to look people in the eye.

There was an old Western TV show called "Branded" that Tony used to watch and that he related to. It was about a cowboy wrongly accused of being a coward. This stain of cowardice followed him through his life and he had to continuously try to clear his name and prove his worth as a man. This story summed up Tony's life to this point. He felt he was more than people could see. He was sure that he would have to spend the rest of his life proving himself because of his father.

Tony's only saving grace was that his paternal grandparents; who lived about a hundred miles away on a farm, and sometimes took him to stay with them for the summer. It was a welcome retreat. He had to help out with chores, but he was fed. He could listen to his grandfather's stories of when he was in the military. This was just about the only thing Tony could look forward to. At the end of the summer he would have to return to Dick and the nightmare would continue.

So many gut-wrenching things happened to Tony that beat him down.

One of Tony's most devastating memories of his childhood happened when he was around eight or nine years old. It was a time when he realized just how poor he was. It seemed like everyone else wasn't, but he was. Tony thought that no matter how old he got he would always remember that day and use it as gravel in his gut for the rest of his life.

The day started out like most. The sun was shining and all the kids from the neighbourhood projects, except the Simons kids, were out playing in front of their houses, like they always did back then during the summer when school was out.

The old man wasn't working, as usual, and there was no food in the house; hadn't been for two days. Tony and his brother and sister were hiding upstairs along with his mother and father because a bill collector was banging on the door. This was a regular occurrence and on this particular day it was the owner of the corner grocery store's turn. It seems he had gotten drunk and decided it was time for Dick to pay his bill. So of course all the kids in the neighbourhood were aware of what was going on and that the Simons were in the house.

The grocery store owner yelled and pounded on the door because he knew they were home. As usual, he finally got tired after awhile and left.

After the bill collector left Dick went over to a neighbour, "Bud" and told him that there was no food in the house and the kids had to eat. It wasn't unusual for Dick to make it seem like he was entitled. When he came back he told Tony and his siblings to grab their bowls and go to Bud's house across the driveway and he would give them something to eat. Tony mustered up the courage to say very emphatically "No! I won't do it!" It didn't mean anything to Dick; he proceeded to smack Tony on the back of his head and kicked him out the door with his bowl. Every kid in the neighbourhood was watching. It was a very traumatic day. They heckled the Simons kids by asking them where they were going and what were they doing with their bowls.

Tony and his siblings walked across the 20 feet to the neighbour's house with all the kids in the neighbourhood watching. The distance felt like a mile.

Three, not so big children, doing at their young age what they knew was wrong, and something parents should not make their kids do. When they finally reached Bud's door, with kindness and a "knowing" he opened a can of beans and dished it out to the shaking kids. Demoralized, hungry and defeated, the kids walked back to their house. The kids in the neighbourhood were still outside, laughing, playing and watching.

Sybil, four year's older, though embarrassed, was callused to these types of experiences. Ronnie, the youngest of the three, not yet old enough to understand, thought it was an adventure and a chance to visit with his friend Bud. Tony was sure this was the worst day of his life. He couldn't imagine it getting any worse, but he was wrong. Dick wasn't through making Tony's life hell.

They moved around a lot in the projects, as much as 10 times in one year. They would move to houses that should have been condemned. Sometimes Dick would make a deal with the landlord to "fix up" the house so as not to have to pay rent.

One such move was outside the projects, to a large fruit farm. It had acres and acres of orchards, including apples, peaches, strawberries, and cherries. There were cottages in one area, about a dozen. Dick made a deal with the owner that the whole Simons family would work the orchards so as not to pay rent. They were slave labour. The problem with that was that Dick was allergic to work and always found a way not to participate. It was going pretty good for awhile, but the old lady found a way to get drunk and took off. There would only be the three kids left to pick the fruit and this did not go well with the farmer. They were out on their ears and back to the projects!

Dick was always two steps ahead of the police and one step ahead of the landlord. Dick liked to "jump rent," doing midnight moves so that the landlord didn't have a chance to collect. After Tony's sister moved away he decided that the family should move to B.C. This he said would be a "new start."

They had a broken down station wagon, which Dick had yet to finish paying for. So the night before they left, he hand-painted it black and with a welfare cheque that was supposed to be used for rent, the baby bonus, and a stolen projector, they were off to B.C.!

Dick was always looking for an angle, always looking for something to "acquire" and sell. The projector got sold along the way for gas money.

When they finally arrived in Vancouver, they were driving on fumes. They had arranged to stay at Darlene's sister, Barb's place with her five kids and alcoholic boyfriend. They lived with this group for almost three months. During this time Dick was able to get back on Welfare.

Barb's boyfriend did not like the arrangement at all and there was more than one fight between the sisters about this. Finally the boyfriend threatened to move out if these free loaders didn't leave. As luck would have it there was an apartment upstairs from Barb's, and Welfare approved the apartment.

Tony was getting older and wiser by now and while in B.C., at 13 years old he was expected to work and handover the money he received to Dick. He had a paper route. He realized that if he wanted something for himself he would have to hide it outside the house. He used some of the money to feed himself. Of course he had to at least give Dick the bare minimum so he wouldn't get suspicious.

Once settled in the new living quarters, it was business as usual. Dick watched TV, Darlene got drunk with her sister; Tony went to school and had his paper route.

A couple of years later things were again not working out, Welfare was going to cut them off because Dick wasn't looking for work, Darlene was not working the program and Dick was making excuses. Dick had been watching Tony and discovered a tin can hidden in a brick pile outside the house that Tony was using to hold the money he had collected from his paper route. Dick then took $200 from the can and said that he'd pay it back. Tony never believed him. Dick wanted the $200 for gas because they were all heading back to the projects! So much for starting over!

For some reason there wasn't enough room in the station wagon for Tony. He wound up travelling in the U-haul that they were carrying behind. Dick put him there because he was fed up with Tony complaining about his "paper route money."

Once they arrived back in Port Nichols, they moved in with Tony's paternal grandmother, Daisy. She had moved into town after Tony's grandfather, Ben passed away the year before while they were in B.C. Tony and his family lived in the basement while Dick looked for another place. Tony's mother and grandmother did not get along at all! Daisy was part native and she wanted Dick to marry a native woman. This is why she despised Tony's mom. Also, Daisy's brother lived on the reservation and would get tobacco and give it to Daisy. Tony's mother helped herself to this and it was also a sore point with Daisy.

Tony found it interesting that he could sit on the step of his grandmother's house and look directly across into the projects.

Chapter 3

In order to understand "the projects" you have to have lived in them and seen them through the eyes of a poor young person. You have to understand why you're there and most importantly, you have to survive them.

The "projects" consisted of block housing, row upon row of two-storey duplexes. It was low rent housing filled with the worker bees of society, trying to eke out a living with low paying jobs. They tried to stay ahead of the bill collectors and the landlords who were raising rent or throwing you out because you didn't pay.

In the back of the housing there would be rows of white laundry on the lines blowing in the dust filled winds from the dredgers that came in from the lakes. Kids played outside, screaming and hollering in common backyards because some little shit hit somebody else and they were telling their moms. Moms screamed at neighbour moms because they didn't know how to raise their monsters correctly, and they should be ashamed of the way their kids were acting. You could hear them screaming at each other above the other sounds of the neighbourhood.

The guys would be under the hoods of old cars in their driveways trying to understand why the thing wasn't working the way it should. All the while listening to two other guys trying to tell the first what they thought was wrong with it and how they thought it should be fixed, while drinking cold beer in their dirty white t-shirts.

Project living was like living in a fish bowl. Everything is seen and talked about. When you enter the projects by turning down a street, or leave your house you are watched and reported on in some way or another. The neighbourhood gossip moves faster than a party line full of old hens after supper. Tony knew this for a fact because he had lived it.

You would think that all that would be enough to not want to live there, but it was even more interesting at night. These neighbourhoods did not sleep even if the kids did. Teenagers hung out on the corners smoking cigarettes or marijuana, sitting on abandoned cars or worse yet, busying themselves in the backseat with a neighbourhood girl who dared venture that way.

There was always a fight going on, if not with the gangs of the neighbourhood or wannabes, it was with any unsuspecting people who got too close to the area at night.

The common backyards also gave way to a host of activity when the sun went down. Women would either be sitting on their back steps talking to someone else two doors down or they would be peering out their upstairs' windows watching for drunken fights that were sure to happen as the evening rolled on. This made for great gossip from their front steps the next morning.

The best stuff happened later on in the evening between 11:00 PM and dawn. This was when the people that were unhappy with their marital situation or thought they could get away with infidelity would become most active. You could see them quietly moving from one house to another in the dark, not turning on any lights or staying long.

With all this going on, nothing was missed by the grannies or cold hearted old biddies that lay in wait for them. They couldn't wait until Sunday so that they could unburden their souls in the confessional as to what was happening in the neighbourhood to the church's flock.

Nothing was left out, everyone was guilty of one sin or another and they were going to make sure that Father Michael was aware of what was happening. Tony could imagine Father Michael looking down from his ivory pulpit calling down the wrath of God on the sinners that he was supposed to be taking care of. Tony pictured the priest as an ancient King looking down from his castle on the hill at his lowly subjects that he believed were not bowing down to him enough or they were not paying him what he deserved. He would make them pay for their sins.

The church ran the projects with an iron fist. Nothing happened there without its' permission. According to Father Michael the people that lived in the projects were peasants that needed a firm hand. They all had to attend church before school and were under the steely watch of the priest's evil army – the nuns. The students quietly referred to them as "penguins" because of their black and white attire.

The nuns were the priest's eyes and ears in the church during the mass and in the school located across the street from Father Michael's castle. The nuns had the students and the weak-minded peasants scared to death. Their word was law when the priest wasn't nearby. Their eyes and ears were always open, trying to catch the students doing or saying something wrong.

If they didn't attend church but showed up at school it was tantamount to treason against the church and Father Michael. The guilty students were stood up straight with their backs against the wall in the hallway and had holes burned into their foreheads by the penguin's evil stares.

They never stopped asking questions about your family and why they were not "good Christians" and why they were not donating more money to the church. They never failed to tell you how generous Father Michael was by giving your family food baskets and chits for shoes so you'd have something to wear;"you ungrateful little beast." The tongue lashing would go on for several minutes until one of them couldn't take it anymore. On one particular occasion Tony pushed the penguin out of his face, thinking that she smelled of bleach. He then ran down the hall screaming that she was an evil person and she should leave him alone. As he ran out of the school he heard her screaming that he was going to hell and was to report to the priest for punishment. He knew this was never going to happen.

The priest was God-like in his own mind and he commanded the penguins to do his bidding whenever it suited him. He would walk down the halls of the school when classes were in and imagined the heathens praying that he did not stop at their classroom. The nuns were especially cruel to the class if he visited, making sure they said nothing. The kids were to stand perfectly still, looking straight ahead. God help you if you twitched. He loved the power he had over them and used it every time he could.

He was especially god-like when he went into the projects to visit his masses and show them how superior he was. He'd call their names out loud if he saw them outside and they would freeze in place until he got to them. The thing Tony hated the most about this sanctimonious bastard was the fact that he would walk into anybody's house at any time of the day or night, just walk in. These uninvited visits scared the hell out of Tony. He'd just walk in and want to know why you were not at school or church and why you were causing trouble for everyone in the projects by complaining.

He'd look into cupboards to see if there was food inside. If he found none, he gave out food chits to the local food store. This act on his part made Tony feel low and dirty and he felt like Father Michael wanted him to kiss his ring.

Tony hated the priest. When Tony found out that the priest had finally been caught and charged with child molestation and interference with a minor, he smiled deeply to himself.

They said that he had been "touching" his alter-boys and the boys complained to their parents. The church moved him quickly and quietly to another parish. No one heard from him again and the nuns never spoke of him after.

The projects were in "riot mode" for some time. The parish and church were constantly being watched by the local police and they had stopped many angry residents from setting the buildings on fire. They wanted the priest. Even though the priest was gone and they couldn't get to him, they wanted to get to the castle. It took a long time for the hate to subside, but it did. Life had to go on in the projects.

Now, sitting on his grandmother's steps, it seemed like an old nightmare.

Chapter 4

Soon after moving in with his grandmother, Tony and his brother settled back into school. Things never change. Everyone in his home school room hated him and knew of his situation at home with his parents and brother. They were never surprised when he didn't show up for class for days at a time. When he did show up he looked tired, dirty and couldn't concentrate, and didn't know what they were talking about. They were never surprised when he told the teacher that he had moved again.

The kids gave up talking to him; he became invisible but he didn't care. One guy in the class knew what he was going through, because he was going through his own kind of hell. Heinz Goble knew about Tony's situation and eventually told him so.

Tony was walking down the hall when Heinz came up behind him and said "never let these bastards break you down Tony; they aren't worth your time. Look them right in the eye and tell them to 'piss off'." He then just walked away.

Who was this guy Tony asked himself. He had seen him in class or in the lunch room sitting alone. He seemed to be blending into the background trying not to be noticed. Heinz Goble became Tony's best friend for the remainder of his time in school.

When they got together, which was often, they talked for hours. Heinz was a big boned, red haired German kid that was taller than Tony by four inches. Heinz's situation was similar to Tony's home life but worse in some respects. Heinz's father beat him a lot, especially when he got drinking his home-made dandelion wine and it was getting worse. Heinz was scared to death and told Tony that he was planning on leaving home soon and he wasn't coming back.

Most of these discussions happened at the Franklin Hotel Bar during lunches that went on for hours. They would get thrown out of class and instead of reporting to the office, they would walk down to the bar to escape the bullshit. Given the boys' size they looked older than they were and the bartender didn't seem to mind or care one way or the other. Tony had the idea that nothing would be said unless they got into trouble.

Even at 15 two things go well together when you need to decompress, cold beer and a game of pool. They played whenever they could and loved the game but weren't very good.

One afternoon when they had little money for beer, Heinz and Tony broke into Heinz's locked cellar at home and took two bottles of dandelion wine that Heinz's old man made. After they finished the wine they decided they would still like to play pool. Heinz mentioned that he heard about a pool hall about a block from the Franklin and they should give that a try.

The pool hall was run by John Dumski, an old Polish man with a thick accent. He was about five feet tall and had about three hairs left on the top of his freckled head and glasses that hung right at the tip of his nose. Rumour had it that John had been there since the place opened up in the 30's and nobody doubted it for a second.

You could always find John in his little office under the stairs that led down from the street. From there he could watch the action on the tables. He watched with his eagle eyes for signs of trouble or hustle from strangers. On this particular afternoon his attention was drawn to two newcomers to the pool hall. He saw two teenagers who were intently walking around the tables and watching the games.

After awhile they went over to a small table located in front of John's office and began to set up. He could see that they were new to the game as they fumbled with balls and cues. They had poor stance and couldn't hold the cue properly. John decided that since it was fairly quiet he would give them a few pointers.

John walked over and introduced himself and the boys in turn told him their names. John knew that these boys were probably missing school, but he didn't press the point. Tony and Heinz were then introduced to the finer points of playing snooker and eight ball by this wily old gentleman who knew his way around a pool table, like Tony and Heinz had never seen before. This man could play.

Not only did he teach them a better game, but he also told them about the history of the pool hall. He said that the pool hall was famous to those who knew where it was and had been at its present location since the 1930's. He said that the pool hall had once been a Speak Easy in the 1930's complete with dancing girls and bathtub booze. He said that it was a true representation of an old prohibition pool hall located under another legendary establishment, the drugstore from the same time period called "Louie's Drugs." The boys were wide-eyed as they listened to the history of the pool hall.

Heinz and Tony played pool for the rest of that afternoon and the evening and from then on it became one of their favourite hangouts. They found that they weren't the only ones that felt that John's was the place you wanted to be on a Saturday night.

Saturday nights it was packed with people playing pool and people watching, waiting to play. There were 12 long tables with worn green velvet tops and the six smaller tables in the same shape were located in front of John's office. These tables could be seen as you came down the stairs.

The floors were well worn, and the smell of cigarettes and cigars assaulted your nose and added to the experience. There were rows of wooden benches, rescued from an old church and were at least 100 years old. They were located along the walls, reserved for the players. If you were lucky, you could find a seat near one of the big tables and watch some great pool.

There was never any alcohol sold at John's place, but you could get a coke and a bag of chips any time you wanted.

A lot of motorcycle club members came there to play on the great tables and respected John's rules about arguing and fighting in the hall. "Take it outside, finish it outside, and then come back in." It was pretty simple.

Tony and Heinz played there for quite some time, but situations change like they tend to and Tony moved again and lost touch with Heinz. He eventually heard from the grapevine that he got caught by his crazy old man in the cellar and was beat so bad that he had to go to the hospital. The last thing Tony heard was that Heinz had ran away from home and no one heard from him again.

Chapter 5

After about six weeks at Tony's grandmother's house, Dick found a place in the area they knew so well, the projects. It was a blur of moves, 30 days here and 30 days there.

As far back as Tony could remember Dick had always had a station wagon. He didn't' own them all the time, sometimes he just "had" them. They were always in some state of repair, good or bad and the tires were usually worn down to the threads, but they usually ran. Tony always thought of them as ugly old land yachts that were as wide as the driveway and as long as a city block.

Tony couldn't drive yet, but he was sure that the proper way to start a car was not by stomping up and down on the gas pedal several times and turning the key until the battery died or the dragon came to life.

Dick would be under the hood on really cold days, pouring lighter fluid or gasoline in some hole at the top of the breathing thing. Then he'd run around to the driver's seat, pound the pedal again and grind the engine until a big blue flame roared from it and the boat would maybe start.

It took Tony the longest time to realize why the old man liked these old dinosaurs so much. It was for the midnight moves. Tony and his family didn't have very much, only the bare essentials really and the old man was a master at getting all their shit into that boat in a hurry if the need arose and often it did.

He never took the big stuff, like the stove or fridge; he could get them from Sally Ann or Goodwill for free, and they delivered! The rest of the crap could be placed strategically in the belly of the beast or on top of the hood and roof.

Tony couldn't believe how three mattresses and a small couch could be tied down on the car roof and a kitchen table, turned upside down could be tied to the hood. Dick would then put boxes inside the table and tie them down. Once loaded to capacity, Dick would move down the street in the middle of the night, with his head sticking out the side window so he could see. Most times the move was not far away and the rest of the family would walk behind the station wagon. The neighbours were none the wiser, and the landlord was on the hook to remove the broken appliances and clean the mess left behind.

Of all the times Tony found himself loading the yacht in the middle of the night only one time brought a smile to his face. The old man tried to teach Tony's mom how to drive the boat so as to help him when needed. Darlene did not drive and didn't want to. Dick didn't care. When he thought he had trained her well enough, he told her to back the beast out of the yard, big mistake. Darlene panicked and gunned the monster in reverse, throwing stones in the air and black smoke from the tail pipe.

Tony remembered her screaming, wide-eyed, mouth open as she barreled down the driveway backwards. She crossed the street and drove into a big ditch on the other side, a deep one. She came to a halt with the back end of the monster deep in the ditch with a broken transmission and the front end up in the air. The engine was still on and the tires were still spinning.'

That was the one and only time Tony's mom ever drove the car.

Nothing changes in the projects, and people just get older. Tony was also getting older, reaching 16 years of age. That spring they moved into a house outside of the projects. The area was known as "The Hill." Now you might think this would be a good thing, but no.

It was one of the worst areas in town. There was a lot of crime and gang violence, drugs; it was a very "active" area. This is where Tony's new home was. Dick didn't really care where they set down; he never seemed to realize the dangerous situations that he put his family in.

This house was a prize. Dick had cut a deal with the landlord so that he didn't have to pay rent again. He actually told the landlord that he could repair the place. It was a four bedroom, two story house, with a lot of the windows smashed out and had been vacant for quite some time. It looked to Tony like it was a place where homeless people or hookers went to stay out of the rain or shoot up. The roof in the dining room was caving from the weight of water that had come in. The plaster of course was long gone. The room above the dining room would be Tony's! Tony's room had a big hole in the ceiling. Lying in bed he could see the stars, and this was kind of cool, but waking up soaked because the rain was coming in was not cool. Tony was very disillusioned by this time and tired of Dick's crap! He had to find a way out!

Chapter 6

Tony Simons was spitting mad. How the hell was he supposed to live in that house! He was 16 years old and feeling like he was done with all of it. He was walking down the street, hands in pockets, head down, long strides, smoking a cigarette. He was tall and a little too thin, long hair covered by an old ball cap. His eyes were blue and filled with determination.

Tony was still trying to go to school. Today, heading home after what seemed a futile day, he'd already decided to quit. He couldn't do it anymore. He couldn't concentrate at school and try to survive at home. The old man's demands that he "find work" were getting worse and worse. He was done.

With his head in a haze, and not paying attention to where he was going he turned down the wrong street, a street not familiar to him. It was in his neighbourhood and on his way home, but he had not been there before. He finally looked up to see rows of three story run-down apartments. It was a mess, with abandoned old cars and kids playing in the street.

Unfortunately Tony had let his guard down. From out of one of the apartment blocks he noticed, too late, that a group of about six determined and crazed looking hoods were heading straight for him. They probably had been watching him from the moment he turned down their street. As soon as they got within striking distance, one of them demanded Tony's cigarettes. Tony, in no uncertain terms, told them to fuck off. Probably the wrong thing to say, but then in this situation what wasn't?

Before he knew it, he was getting beaten to an inch of his life. They were all on him. They got him down and put their boots to him. They wanted to know who the hell he thought he was coming down their street!

In Tony's estimation, it seemed to go on forever. Everything seemed to slow down. At some point Tony covered his head to shield it. When he finally looked up he suddenly saw one of the guys standing over him jerk back and fall to the ground. Tony was confused and as the hoods changed their focus it gave Tony an opportunity to stand up and start fighting back again.

Street fighting is dirty fighting, no rules, anything goes. The goal is to inflict pain quickly. It doesn't take much to end a fight either, a lucky punch or a kick in the groin usually does it. Tony was able to land a finishing blow to the noisy one that had demanded his cigarettes. Two of the other guys were already on the ground. It was then that Tony finally noticed his rescuer, Mark. He wondered where the heck he came from and who the hell he was.

It was then that the group decided it wasn't worth the battle and backed off. They began shouting threats at Tony and Mark, waving their fists, and telling them never to come down their street again!

Tony was grateful that Mark had shown up and saved his ass. Tony knew of him and his family, Mark only lived down the street from Tony, but they had never really met until now.

Tony came away with bruises, torn clothes and a bloody nose; in fact they both looked very much alike at that point, but Tony still had his cigarettes.

They continued walking until they got to Mark's house, sat on the steps, took a few deep breaths, and discussed the fight in detail. The story was akin to "the one that got away." They spoke with a new-found common ground. They spoke about how the guys they had just fought with got away lucky because Mark and Tony were just getting started.

Mark wanted to know why Tony had ventured down that particular street. Tony told him about home, that he was thinking of leaving school and that he couldn't really take it anymore. He said that he was caught up in thinking about all of that when he happened to turn down the wrong street.

Tony knew that Mark was a better fighter than he, but for now, they basked in the commonality neither one had had before.

Tony and Mark started hanging out after that, and they decided they could watch one another's backs. They both had younger brothers that would probably need protecting as well.

Mark had already quit school and Tony quit shortly after that day. School was a joke. They had no idea what was going on outside of the school doors, or they refused to acknowledge it. It was easy for someone like Tony to become disillusioned. He thought at one point that education might be his way out, but at least for now, he was sure it wasn't going to happen that way. So now, he was on a stoop with a new friend, and a new chapter at last.

Chapter 7

The Burns family of Port Nichols could trace their family back to before this prosperous city had the enormous harbour area that became home to so many different vessels from different lands. Many of the immigrants that came to Ontario were farmers that would work the lands and grow fruit. Investors came with them and brought new money to build factories that would hire more new people. They would land there from England, Ireland, Germany and Italy.

The Burns family, Thomas, his wife Victoria, and three boys; Shamus, Mickey and Thomas Junior were on one of these boats that landed there to call it home. Times were hard back then but the Burns family was old-world Irish and tough as they come. Hard work had not been a stranger to them and it didn't take long for Thomas to find work on the dockyards.

Thomas brought his family's old-world ideas with him. He was the man of the family, and his word was law, as his father's were before him. It was hard back then and everyone had to pull their weight to make things work. Police were called many times to Thomas' house. Records show that Thomas did not stand for laziness and disobedience from his family. This was met by a stern, hard hand. No one in their family was exempt from Thomas' punishment. Even his loving wife Victoria, medical records would show, had been beaten regularly. People went on police record stating that she was always the centre of his anger when things were not going his way at work, or when he had too many drinks at the local pub.

Victoria was a survivor and she put up with her lot in life for 35 years and three children. She stayed with Thomas and put up with the beatings only to protect the children from him, but she was tired. She wondered how long she could go on knowing that a deep pain in her chest was getting worse and tapping her strength. That final year she hoped she could make it to summer.

One evening Thomas came home in one of his blind rages looking for supper that wasn't there. Victoria was lying in their bed, trying to rise, when she heard him coming in. She hadn't moved most of the day but she knew her boys were old enough to watch themselves. Thomas roared and called her a lazy bitch and she was going to pay for not looking to his meal. He grabbed her before she could rise and shook her into unconsciousness. She never recovered.

Reports taken from neighbours showed that he had been heard screaming at her at first, then crying out loud for help. Thomas was immediately charged with murder and jailed to await trial. The boys were put in the care of a friend's family, Tommy Portland, and his wife Martha, while the trial was going on.

Later medical records showed the poor woman had suffered from advanced Tuberculosis. The records cleared Thomas of this awful miscarriage of justice and he was released to care for his boys.

This didn't happen at all. Thomas went into a deep depression and drank every day. He had lost his job on the docks after being arrested and wound up unloading bean sacks from coffee merchant ships. The boys spent most of their time on the streets of Port Nichols, hustling newcomers out of their money, and stealing food when they could find it. They stayed clear of Thomas when they could.

A year or so later Thomas Junior passed away from a short bout of pneumonia, trying to live on the streets and surviving Thomas' beatings.

Thomas' drinking eventually led to him becoming ill. Shamus was trying to take care of his sick father and be a brother to Mickey at the same time. This too fell apart when Mickey was caught stealing from a garment factory, trying to stay warm. He was sent to a work farm for many years.

By then Shamus was a 19 year old man and Thomas was near dead from liver problems. He spent so much time watching over Thomas, he forgot to look around and see that things were changing and he was getting older.

He eventually got a job in one of the new factories in the machine shop and vowed never to give up this chance to do better.

A 20 year old Shamus found that he was alone, when Thomas passed away leaving nothing behind but the bad memories of an angry, unloved, lonely old man.

Shamus concentrated on his work and getting ahead the best he could. He owed no one. One thing bothered him every day; he was alone. He had made a few friends at work but when he was at home, he was alone. His friends tried to get him to meet ladies but Shamus was untrained in the art of meeting girls and avoided them entirely.

One grey day an accident happened in the shop and it cost a man his life. Grief came over the shop and the funeral was even worse. The man was a year younger than Shamus at only 25 and he left behind a young wife, Olive and her son Skip. They were alone, just like him. This set Shamus to wondering if he could help the family and hopefully strike up a friendship with them in their time of need.

In the following weeks and months, Shamus watched them and offered help whenever possible. Over time a friendship rose between Shamus and Olive. Skip began to look to him also. The couple talked constantly about their situations and Shamus began to spend more and more time with this lonely woman.

Skip looked at Shamus and saw a big friendly man that made his mother smile for the first time in a long while. Olive looked at Shamus and saw security in hard-times, and a father-figure for her son. Skip was four going on five years old and needed a strong hand to guide him.

They eventually married and had five more children, two boys and three girls.

In the time that followed Shamus became more hostile to Skip; after all, he really wasn't his. He beat him regularly, complaining to Olive about "her son" not pulling his weight. Skip did not want to work with Shamus in his shop. This made Shamus very angry.

Shamus Burns was well over six feet and weighed about 300 pounds. He had short salt and pepper hair. He was a big man with big hands. He was also very loud. You could pretty much hear him streets away, especially when he was drinking.

Shamus was becoming more and more like his father everyday and blamed any troubles they were having on Olive and her lazy son. He was drinking more and getting into more fights at the pub, sometimes landing him in jail. He began hitting Olive during these drunken rages, just as his father had done to Victoria before him. The difference was that Skip would defend his mother and threaten to beat him if he did not stop attacking his mother.

When the fighting was going on, the kids would take off. At times he would stay away on a drinking binge and when he did, Mark stuck around more. No one knew why Olive stayed. Eventually, she did wind up leaving.

Skip's half brother, Mark, watched the way Shamus treated his mother and older half brother and hated him for it. Skip would tell Mark that someday, he would make Shamus pay.

Tony thought that Mark's family was "interesting."

Mark, like Tony, was tall and lanky, but he towered over him at 6'8. He was always trying to prove how tough he was because he was so thin and appeared weak because of it. He wore his hair short, and that was because his old man wouldn't let him grow his hair. He had dark brown eyes and a narrow nose and always had a serious, challenging look about him. He wore dirty blue jeans, and favoured a black hooded shirt and work boots. He didn't talk much, but when he did you could see the broken teeth on one side of his mouth from the many fights he had been in.

He belonged to a tough family and had to prove himself all the time, inside the family and out. Problems came when anyone mentioned Mark's size. His fights were full out, not just one punch and he kept breaking his hands. He always seemed to have something broken.

Mark's family was well-known in the town. They were "Black Irish" and had lived in town forever. They were a very tough group, because Mark's Dad, Shamus, ran his family with an iron fist. There was no discussion. It was his way and his way only.

There were three boys and three girls in the family. They had to be as tough as the old man; he wouldn't have it any other way. They were taught to take no shit from anybody.

Olive was tall and thin, Tony thought of her as looking like a barnyard chicken, "Miss Prissy" came to mind. She was a super lady, kind, and kept the house together. Her house was always open to the lost souls of the neighbourhood.

The three girls in the family stayed close together at school and if one of them happened to get into trouble with anyone, the other two were not far away and willing to jump in.

Mark's younger brother, Billy was the smallest of the three boys; he was smart, liked school and did well there. Even at a young age he was destined to do more with his life. Olive was going to see to that.

Then there was Skip, Mark's half-brother. He was as tall as the rest of the boys in the family, about 6'3, and gaunt. He was thicker than his half brother with sharp facial features, brown eyes and short hair. He had big hands and was hard as steal and twice as tough. He was about six years older than Mark.

Mark knew that Skip took after his natural father because Olive talked to Skip at length about his him and how much he reminded her of him. He was proud when she looked at him and he could see her thinking of his late father. To protect him, she would give him money to stay away from the house when she knew that Shamus was on a bender. Skip hated Shamus and he knew that this would end badly.

He constantly fought with Shamus until he found a group of like-minded people, survivalists, and left home. He was probably the only one that the old man feared. He was able to survive on the street so no one was surprised when he left home. The survivalist group turned out to be a bike club known as Lucifer's Army. It wasn't long before he became the Sergeant At Arms for the club. Skip's exploits were well known in the streets. He was dangerous and not to be trifled with.

Chapter 8

Now that neither Tony nor Mark was going to school they had the time to look for work. What the hell can we do to make money? This had to be their number one priority. Tony and Mark took stock of themselves. They were a couple of high school dropouts with no skills and no prospects for the future. They couldn't go to Mark's old man because Mark would probably get an earful and a kick in the ass and he didn't want to work with his dad anyway. Going to Dick was a total waste of time, Tony would never ask for help from that asshole!

They walked downtown the next day, and found themselves in front of the Unemployment Building. They knew that new jobs were posted just inside the door, but you had to register in order to get more information. There was also a billboard just to the left of the front door and men were milling around it. They seemed to be taking notes and moving away.

They were mostly young men but there was also a few older mixed in. Tony could see that most were new to Canada and to Port Nichols. They were in small groups talking quietly amongst themselves and shaking their heads. Tony could see that at least one in the group spoke English and was explaining to the others what they were looking at on the boards. They nodded their heads and thanked the man that was interpreting. Tony thought that he was probably a cousin or something as he watched the group climb into a Chevy van and drive away.

With the board clear of people now, Tony and Mark could see what they had been looking at. It was a day-labourers' work board. The board listed construction sites and farms in the area that required people to work for them on a daily basis to fill in where full time people were not required. Workers were paid daily, by the hour or in the case of fruit picking, by the piece. Piece work meant that you were paid to fill baskets with fruit and were paid by the number of baskets you filled by the end of the day. Hourly workers could make from $1.30 to $1.60 per hour depending on what the job was and how long they wanted you.

Tony read the job openings aloud trying to get an idea as to what they could do. Construction sites in the city needed general labourers for day work only. They had to be physically fit and have work boots. Parks needed clean-up workers to remove garbage from baseball and football fields. Street sweepers were needed in the downtown core to keep the sidewalks clean. Finally, fruit pickers were needed in a number of farm areas to pick anything from apples to strawberries, not to mention grape cutting. All of the positions were outside in the hot sun. Being young and invincible, Tony and Mark could see several easy ways to make quick cash.

They decided to try construction because the money was better and they could get work boots from Mark's garage. The notice said to be in front of the bulletin board every morning at 6:00 AM and a foreman driving a truck would pick the guys he wanted. This was the main pickup site for all the day jobs.

Tony and Mark thought they struck gold. If they had money coming in every day, how hard could it be? It didn't take long for the boys to realize what manual labour meant, all day every day back breaking work. They moved wheelbarrows full of concrete to and from holes in the ground. When they weren't hauling concrete they were on the end of a shovel digging some useless hole. Later the boys found out that this type of work was called "riding a goon spoon." They were not impressed!

After a week or so, the novelty of construction wore off and the small pay at the end of the day wasn't near enough to make it worthwhile and the guys decided to look for a new career.

Picking fruit, it had to be easier than construction. They would find out that it could be damn hard if you didn't know what you were doing. They'd need a hat, a big one because it was hot out there. Being out all day, going up and down a ladder in the mid day sun carrying baskets can be completely draining.

Tony knew his day was going to be shitty when he woke at the crack of dawn and found it was raining like hell out. The orchards were not going to be kind, but this was his new career after all. Mark needed hazard pay on days like these, because he kept falling off the slippery ladders and dumping his fruit all over the ground. This got him into a lot of shit because there was always a boss around when he took the big dive into the mud. Tony wasn't much better off, being soaked to the bone. Piece work was no way to keep yourself fed, let alone have enough money at the end of a shitty day to have a beer.

"Strawberries, let's try strawberries." This too was a mistake. It was over a hundred degrees in the patches, bent over and physically dying of dehydration while you hunted the little bastard berries. One thing about Port Nichols, there was always fruit to be picked and the guys moved on to yet another new adventure.

They were going to cut grapes. They were still outside and still at the mercy of the weather, but it was somewhat easier on the back and legs and you could take a break anytime you needed to. If they planned it right, Tony and Mark could work in the next row over from each other and they could talk all day about their future while they worked.

When you get a lot of people in the fields all at once you hear a lot about how other workers are holding up and what they're doing to find better jobs, full time jobs. This is what was happening this one fine sunny morning when Tony and Mark found themselves just over from a small group of new Canadians that were talking about the nearby winery. They said that they had heard that the processing plant was looking for an extra crew and they would be hiring at the end of the summer. Tony looked at Mark and their eyes got wide with excitement. This is what they had been looking for. At the end of the day, over a beer, they planned their next move.

When Tony's old man found out that he was working, he told Tony in no uncertain terms that he would be paying rent. Tony was disgusted and told his old man so. This earned him a slap on the back of the head.

Chapter 9

When they weren't working they did what most teenagers did – they went for beers!

The local watering hole was called "The Franklin Hotel." It was located in the seedier part of town, not far from where Mark and Tony lived. It was a large, old two-storey building, located at an intersection with four corners. It was built in the 30's and had a lot of character. There was nothing special about the outside façade, just grey stone and it was built right up next to the street.

Once inside you could smell stale cigarettes, and beer and all the wild parties that had gone by previously. Inside it was alive. It had a big round bar and large old booths up against the wall and long tables in the middle of the floor. The tables were covered with cigarette burns, water rings and carved initials, names and dates. Some of which were probably no longer around.

If you listened carefully, you could hear some of the stories told by the old bartender. The bartender's name was Mo Tuddle. His real name was Maurice, but no matter how much you drank, you didn't dare call him that. He was big, thick and about 60 years old. He was an ex-biker who didn't take any shit from anyone. He had a big booming laugh that filled the bar. He poured a really good beer and never short-changed you on a shot. He probably heard every sob story there was from just about everyone who frequented the establishment. It didn't seem to matter to Mo, that some of his patrons were not quite of legal age. When things got heated, as they often did, Mo had help in the form of a gun and a bat he kept under the bar. He had no problem using either one. Most times just the sight of them would settle things down.

A stairway led upstairs, separating a pool/games area and a small stage. It was made of very old oak, painted dark brown. It had cigarette burns on the first railing post that curved up. Most of the guys would put their cigarettes out before heading on upstairs with one of the girls. The stairs always squeaked and they were covered with very old, worn, flowered carpet.

The main area itself was always dimly lit and a little on the cold side. The floors were plank wood. It was hard to imagine how much beer got spilled between the floor boards. There was a jukebox that always played during the week because there was always lots of people there putting quarters in.

On the weekend the place rocked with loud live music of one sort or another. Sometimes there were strippers or local talent shows. Tony and Mark thought this place was heaven.

One Friday night, everyone was getting loaded and having a blast. There would be a stripper entertaining on the stage. Tony and Mark were finally lucky enough to get a table near the stage. On this particular night the stripper wasn't really attractive to look at but she moved around pretty good. She happened to glance over to Tony and motion to him to join her on the stage. All the guys were laughing, and Tony was a little embarrassed by the whole thing but he went ahead and joined her. She danced around Tony, stopped in front of him and lowered her top so as to give Tony a better look. She looked Tony in the eye and told him to tell the audience how many he saw. At this point Tony had a sloppy grin on his face, looked down her shirt and held out three fingers to the crowd. Everybody in the bar broke into mad laughter; the stripper howled and hit Tony on the back of the head. Tony returned to his table and drank a bunch of beer! It was a great night and Mark told Tony he was his hero!

Upstairs there was a cat house. Girls would work the floor propositioning the guys and lead them up the staircase. There was usually a guard posted at the bottom of the stairs. This guard was usually a biker belonging to the bike club, Lucifer's Army. The bar was owned by a little Italian guy named Jo, short for Joseppi, but it, as well as the cat house was controlled by Lucifer's Army. There were a lot of paychecks spent here.

There were a lot of fights at the Franklin Hotel for one reason or another. Some ensued because someone tried to rough up one of the girls. It was quite the establishment. It could be a quiet night in the street, but as soon as you walked through the door, it was a different world.

Chapter 10

With Tony and Mark spending time at the Franklin Hotel most nights, they got to know a lot of the guys who also came in a lot. One of these guys was Lenny, a shy farm kid, blond hair, blue eyes, and muscular. He was very polite and very mild mannered. Lenny's pride and joy was a bright red 1954 Chevy. It had a powerful engine and was really fast. He wasn't used to drinking a lot, but on this particular night he was tanked. When Lenny got drinking he liked to talk about his car.

He was telling everyone how fast it was and everyone was listening whether they wanted to or not. Skip (Mark's brother) happened to be at the bar this evening and heard everything that Lenny was saying. Skip had a really fast 1963 Mustang, stripped down and moved like a rocket. He and Lenny got into an argument about how fast their cars were. They got pretty heated about it. Lenny called Skip out to see who had the fastest car, and wanted everyone to know about it.

Tony was looking at the 54 Chevy; he knew it was a really nice piece of work and of course so was Skip's. They were going to drag the cars. They were going to take the cars out a half mile and race them to the intersection where the Franklin Hotel was. Everyone from the Franklin Hotel was now in the intersection, all drunk.

Lenny's car was mainly engine and body; light, very light. Lenny wanted some extra weight in the back end to put traction on the tires, so Tony and Mark got in the back seat. It was the stupidest thing they'd ever done, they could have died.

The cars cruised out to the half mile marker and turned around. Someone staged the cars so the race would be fair. Engines were revving, cars were shaking and rocking. The starter gave them the go ahead and they took off. Tony thought it was like riding a rocket through hell.

Up to this point Lenny had babied his car. They were pretty sure he'd never driven it so fast. It was insane! Somehow Skip got out in front and sped past them. They were getting closer to the four way stop in front of the Franklin Hotel. Just about a 100 yards out Lenny's car was really moving, Tony felt everything was a blur. There were no seat belts, which made the ride even more interesting for Tony and Mark. Lenny was screaming his face off, looking straight ahead, and hands gripping the wheel.

Skip crossed the line about a half a block ahead of Lenny. There was a massive audience of drunks yelling and howling. Though he was normally a quiet kid, Lenny went nuts because he knew he had lost. He didn't stop at the finish line. He kept going and turned the steering wheel a bit and hit the curb. The car launched just before the intersection and was up off the ground. They literally flew through the intersection.

There was a small store on the corner, across from the intersection. The car landed, bounced and flew right into the store window. The car came to rest passing through the window and landing against the back wall, surprisingly not making it through the wall.

There was a lot of noise as the car crashed. People started yelling; it was a real mess. Some people were laughing, like drunks do! Other people jumped into the window and tried to get the doors of the car open. Lenny got busted up pretty bad, hitting the steering wheel. Both wrists were broken; his face was cut badly, and he had lost some teeth. His car was a total write off.

Tony and Mark were in the back seat on the floor, which padded the impact somewhat. They mainly had bumps and bruises and had a shocked look on their faces. But when they were yanked out of the car, some guys from the crowd called them "crazy sons of bitches."

The cops and the ambulance were called in and it took them forever to get there. A couple of the guys from the bar got Lenny out and laid him on the sidewalk. Once the cops arrived the car was hauled out of the store and the boys got hauled to the station for statements. Awhile later they were released in their fathers' care. They never saw Lenny again after that night.

They were the talk of the town for the next couple of weeks. When they returned to the bar, there was a lot of back slapping and stories about the race. Tony and Mark were folk heroes for awhile. Skip came over to their table and congratulated the boys on the size of their balls, while laughing and commiserating about the whole sequence of events.

Skip, as brothers do, told Mark not to be so stupid ever again or he'd have to kick his ass. Mark told him it wouldn't be as easy as he thought and Tony would be helping him as well. They all laughed.

Tony was still going home most nights, but he was really pissed when he found out that his parents would go through his pants at night, looking for money and cigarettes. Then he realized that not only was he paying rent, but they were still receiving welfare for him and getting a baby bonus!!!! Tony was blind with anger! He threw Dick against the wall and told him he wasn't going to take his shit any longer.

As soon as he left he called the Welfare Department and turned him in. He knew he wouldn't be going back. He knew he was capable of a whole lot more. When he found out what Tony had done, Dick was fit to be tied, according to Ronnie. He found out that Tony had called Welfare. There would be no Welfare cheques, no baby bonus and no rent coming in from Tony! His meal ticket was gone.

Tony went to Mark's house and since his mom was used to taking in strays, Tony had a place to stay.

Chapter 11

Since the night of the race and the nickname of "crazy
bastards" it seemed that Mark and Tony were accepted more
and more into the group of Skip and his biker friends at the
Franklin. Whenever Mark and Tony walked into the bar and
members of Skip's club were there, someone would
invariably yell "hey you crazy bastards! Get over here and
have a beer!"

This particular night started out like most week nights
did. Sitting around the table, shooting the shit about what
happened the day before. The conversation slowly moved its
way around to the fight that Mark and Tony had had on that
forbidden street a few weeks previously. Skip usually knew
everything that was going on, but hearing about this now
really pissed him off.

He wanted to know how it happened and why they had
been there. They told him that a group of thugs had jumped
Tony and Mark, who was close by, heard the scuffle, and

stepped in to help. Skip wanted to know who these assholes were and talked about paying them a visit.

Skip wasn't only Mark's brother but he was also the Sergeant at Arms of one of nastiest motorcycle gangs in the city. The fact that his little brother was getting beat on by some street hoods he didn't take kindly to, especially so close to home. He was going to find out more about these assholes and everybody could see he was taking this personal, an affront. He said "they will die, and that will take care of it."

The following week, Skip and about five other bikers were at the Franklin getting loud and pissed. You could see that something was brewing but no one was aware of what that might be. Tony and Mark were there as well, but sitting with another small group.

Suddenly, it got very loud, then really quiet. Skip and two other guys approached Tony and Mark's table. They told Tony and Mark that "they were going for a ride." Tony was thinking that this was cool. He'd never been on a motorcycle before, and certainly not with a gang member.

It was a very heady experience; Tony never dreamed he'd ride second seat on a "Lucifer's Army" motorcycle. He was on a 1000 cc Sportster Harley, reconverted. It was really loud, throaty, and very powerful. The kind of sound a boy's wet dream was made of. Tony didn't think he was going to be able to hold on. He didn't know where to put his hands. He wasn't sure he should be grabbing the big bad biker by his waist or his belt.

The monster driving this bike was called "Meat." Tony didn't think he should ask why. He didn't say much, didn't need to. He just motioned Tony to get on. He wore a bandana on his skinned head, and had the best looking mustache Tony had ever seen.

Mark rode with a biker named Danny Teacher, born on a motorcycle and deadly with a knife.

The six bikes all fired up were impressive on their own but when you get these big nasty tough men on them, well it makes quite a picture. Exhaust filled the air.

Tony and Mark didn't know where they were going. Skip led out and all the others followed. Tony hung on for dear life, not knowing just how to do it. All that kept going through his mind was "now what?" His first time on such a bike was amazing, scary and exciting all at the same time. It was amazing to Tony how this biker controlled this huge machine. Turning corners and curves in the road was like a dance.

The ride took place late at night, about 11:00 PM, and people on the street would stop what they were doing and watch as the bikers drove by. After awhile, Tony started to think they were turning back to the Franklin. They got back to the four corners in front of the hotel, but then made a left turn and headed down to where the boys lived. Tony was puzzled by then; the bikes went passed his street. They went two more streets up and didn't they wind up on the street where the fight took place!

Tony didn't know what was going to happen. He thought maybe they were going to war. They drove right down to where the fight occurred and parked their bikes right in front of the apartment building. Skip didn't say a word; he just lined the bikes up on the curb, and revved their engines for what seemed to be an eternity, gunning the piss out of them. Every window in the apartment building was dark. You could feel all their eyes glaring at them from the windows, watching while the six bikers gunned their engines, daring them to come out.

After a while, they idled down the engines and told Tony and Mark to get off the bikes and stand in front of them for a minute or two. They didn't say a word; they did as they were told. They stood in front of the bikes, staring at the building. After what seemed to be an eternity, Skip told them to get back on the bikes and they drove slowly away.

They drove to Mark's house, no one spoke and the bikes drove away.

Every now and then Tony and Mark saw the guys they had fought with, but now there was a very quiet understanding between them.

Chapter 12

Finally, it was the end of the summer and the winery was hiring. They were adding a new shift, so Mark and Tony headed over. They were looking for about 18 guys, so it wasn't difficult for them to get in. It was hard work and low pay, but it was full time.

The boys wound up in the press, and in the laundry. Tony worked at the bottom of the press, in the "pit." You really had to be there to truly understand just how bad it was. It was a big hole, 6' by 6' square, 20 feet deep, and the only source of light was that which came in from the top of the hole.

A 6' by 6' rack was put on top of the grate and four Italian workers would place a blanket on top of the rack. Grape mash would be poured on top of the blanket; the four guys would fold the cloth in on itself to hold the grape mixture. They would then put another rack on top, and the whole process would be repeated until there was a total of 20 stacked racks. When this was done, they would operate a press that would come down on the racks and would squeeze all the juice out of the grapes. This would leave nothing but pulp in the cloth.

They would then lift up the press and move the rack to another area where it was stripped down. Once the pulp was shaken out of the cloth, it was thrown into the wash area and that is where Mark would pick them up and put them in an industrial washer. Once washed, he would pile them next to the press.

Tony climbed down a ladder, 20 feet into the hole. His job was to keep the grate at the bottom of the pit clear so that the juice could run down the walls and then converge into the centre of the pit where the juice could go into the system and into the plant to be turned into wine.

Tony's job was a dirty one, but what made it worse was that because the Italians didn't like anyone else working in the winery, they would kick extra mash down the hole so that it would hasten the clogging of the grate where Tony worked like mad trying to keep it clear.

Not long after they started working at the winery, Tony and Mark found out what the Italians were up to and one day met up with four of them in the washroom where they voiced their displeasure in a physical way. The fight didn't

last long, it was probably a draw, but Mark and Tony stood their ground and told them that they better get used to it because they weren't going away. Things settled down after that.

Working at the winery had some perks. At the end of a shift the boys would each get a bottle of wine. They would drink the wine on their way to their favourite watering hole, in time for last call.

Chapter 13

Before Tony met Mark, he knew about Skip's motorcycle club. The club was just down the street from the Franklin, just across the river. He'd seen them around town and heard about the scuffles they had with other clubs. It never crossed his mind that he might at some point become a member.

Tony and Mark had a habit of getting into fights at the bar, mostly "just because." It didn't take much. It didn't take a lot to set someone off. People from outside the area would come in to use the facilities of the cathouse. No one liked strangers in the neighbourhood watering hole. A couple of members of the club were close to a couple of the girls that worked upstairs and they didn't take kindly to outside people butting in to their territory. So by association, Mark and Tony also got into fights. Especially while sitting with club members, which they did more and more these days.

At some point in the new relationship between the boys and the bikers they were invited to the clubhouse when the bar was closing. They could continue drinking and having a good time, as long as they didn't get involved with club business. They were considered "visitors."

The boys, being only 17, thought that it was an honour, being invited into the inner sanctum. The first time they walked in, they were each given a beer, a slap on the back as welcome and told to pull up a chair. The boys couldn't help gawking at everything.

The clubhouse was situated under a high level bridge, tucked back at the end of a road, up against a park. It was heavily treed, and you wouldn't know it was there unless you really looked. It was originally an old blanket factory. It was a huge building with two stories made of brick and had a big walled courtyard where trucks once parked. The motorcycles were parked in the yard outside now and in the ground floor of the building. There were no windows on the main floor making it very secure on the inside.

Security cameras could be seen everywhere in the courtyard. The only way into the courtyard was by large sliding steal doors. They were about 15 feet high and very imposing. There was no way over the walls. The corners of the courtyard were lit by large flood lights. The club members did a lot of chopping and working on their motorcycles on the ground floor of the clubhouse where there were work areas set up in the corners.

The 2nd floor was a huge common area, with one large window that overlooked the courtyard. The common area consisted of a couple of pool tables, a large well-stocked bar, some tables for hanging out, a couple of televisions, and a couple of pinball machines. Off to one side there was a large meeting table. The walls were plastered with pictures of motorcycles. There was a motor on an engine stand over by one of the pool tables. A long hall at the back had three or four bedrooms attached to it. Some of the guys would crash there because they were between places to live, or they would bring their girlfriends there for some privacy.

Every clubhouse has a resident badass. Now you might think that it would be the Sergeant at Arms or the head biker bitch, but you'd be wrong. It was a crow! The guys had acquired a big black crow from somewhere. It had a split tongue and could curse like a drunken sailor. Anyone coming near the crow's cage was subject to his fury especially someone new. They named him Satan and his name suited him. Tony and Mark were not ready for the greeting in the form of a tongue lashing they got from Satan.

At the end of the night Tony and Mark agreed that it had been the best experience they'd had up until then.

Chapter 14

The bikers held most of their club meetings in the common room of the clubhouse and Mark and Tony were not allowed to attend for some time to come.

Some of the club members had regular jobs, and families and they were part owners in the clubhouse itself. Some of their income came from doing business with factories in the area where club members would "acquire" and make deals for items like booze and cigarettes. Because they were so close to the border, a lot of this material was also coming across nightly, unobserved. Money was definitely coming in. Along with a little side-line business in pot and girls, they managed to do quite well.

A lot of the bikes they drove were built and repaired with parts acquired from the states and anywhere else they could get their hands on them. They would sell most of the parts that they didn't use to add to their monetary base.

There were as many as 40 club members at any given time. Some members came and went, but there was always a pretty steady core.

The President of the club was Kevin Donley. He was very smart and his day job was in town in a trucking company. The club was Kevin's dark side. He was able to have another life where he could do so many things he didn't dare do in his business life. He was pretty high up in the trucking company and had access to information helpful to the club.

Kevin was a big man; he wore a beard and short hair. He was quiet but very direct. No one messed with him. If there was something to be done, he got it done. He was mostly even keeled, but he did have a bad temper once provoked. No one wanted to be on the receiving end of that temper.

The Vice President was Rick Fables. This was a hard-core biker, who had been patched to another club long ago but Tony didn't know which one and never asked. Rick lived at the club house. He was a dangerous man, not to be messed with either. If he liked you it was great and life was good. If you messed up, it was not a good day for you. He was totally loyal to Kevin.

Rick and Skip were very tight. They were the authority in the club. They carried out orders that came from Kevin at any given time.

When Lucifer's Army felt like getting away to party for a weekend when the weather was warm, they liked to go to International Beach. It was close to Niagara Falls and the United States Border and was a favourite location for a lot of motorcycle clubs from all over. This beach was supposed to be neutral territory. No one club had claimed it as their own. That wasn't to say that they liked bumping into each other there which was way too often.

It just so happened that this day a rather large motorcycle gang out of Niagara Falls called the "Lone Wolves" and Lucifer's Army decided to hang out at the beach on the same day. The beach area was very large and the chance of both clubs running into each other at the very same place was remote. But not today!

When the Army arrived, they noticed that the Lone Wolves were already there. They weren't too concerned because other than a few small scuffles and bar fights, there hadn't been any real heartache between these two clubs for quite some time.

The Army brought in 42 motorcycles and it takes a large area to park that many bikes. Along with the bikes, Mark and Tony had driven a van which carried a bunch of beer. They also parked near the Army. It turned out that the Army had to park near the Lone Wolves' parking area. Along with all the club bikes there were also a lot of other people at the beach, their vehicles parked in the parking lot as well and most of them were enjoying the amusement park at one end of the beach.

Once parked, the Army got off their bikes and headed for the beer tent. They were just coming out of the parking lot, not noticing that the Lone Wolves had left three guys behind to watch their bikes. They didn't take kindly to the Army being there, let alone how close they were parked.

The three started walking over to Kevin, who hadn't made it out of the parking lot yet. They were throwing insults and challenges at him. Skip moved closer to Kevin, while the Wolves started yelling "what are you bastards doing here? You should all fuck of!" The Lone Wolf bikers walked directly into the midst of the Army. It was easy to see there was going to be a fight.

One of the Wolves picked his foot up and kicked over one of the Army's bikes. Things immediately went from bad to worse. Kevin, Rick and Skip went ballistic. No one touches an Army's ride! The three Wolves were no match for Kevin, Rick and Skip. They beat them into the ground and looked for more.

People were screaming and howling. Someone had notified security. While this was happening, the other Wolves heard the yelling and fighting and returned to the parking lot to be sure their bikes were ok. They saw the Army and their three guys on the ground. The rest of the Army decided to follow suit and kicked the Wolves' bikes down which started an all out war.

It was brutal. The clubs didn't like each other. No one touches another guy's bike. It was tantamount to spitting in your mother's eye.

It felt like it lasted forever, but really only lasted about 10 minutes or so. There is nothing like a bunch of pissed off bikers.

Mark and Tony were trying to hold their own. They weren't wearing any colours or patches yet, but they were fighting the best they could, throwing kicks and punches at anybody that came near them. They were guilty by association.

There were a lot of people down, knocked out or hurt. The girls that ride with these bikers are nasty bitches. They are cut from the same cloth and they fight alongside one another.

Suddenly things stopped, like someone had blown a whistle. There was a very large crowd watching the battle.

Park security was there, but what could they do, they didn't make enough money to mess with these guys. The Police hadn't shown up yet.

Soon after, the Army got on their bikes and left. They weren't sure what the Wolves were going to do. It didn't matter, because the Army got stopped on the highway heading back to town. Everyone had to give statements and the police talked to Kevin for quite some time before they took him in, since he was responsible for his club.

A couple of Lucifer's Army also got arrested. There were fines for disturbing the peace, but no one laid any real charges. There is a code even between rival clubs.

Everyone else went back to the clubhouse and partied for the rest of the night. No one seemed to care that they weren't at the beach.

Chapter 15

Things settled down and became routine for awhile after the lake fiasco. Mark and Tony went to work at the winery, and spent more and more off time with the bike club at the clubhouse or at the Franklin.

One night, after having a particularly grueling day at the winery, they were at the Franklin playing pool, laughing, and putting a comedic spin to the day. Skip and three other guys were there. Things were pretty layback and everyone seemed to be having a good time.

There was a bigger than normal crowd at the bar that evening. The tables were full of guys laughing, drinking and getting loud about some shit or another. Mark didn't recognize any of them. He asked Tony if he knew anyone and he said that he didn't. They continued with their game.

One table seemed to be noisier than the rest. Tony was aware of the noise, but didn't think much about it. Skip was joking about Tony playing like a girl, and making comments about the different shots. Tony wasn't bothered because he was winning and he didn't care. Tony cleared the table on his last three shots, won the game, and declared he was thirsty. With that, they moved over to the bar, pool cues in hand.

"Hey Mo" Tony shouted. "Mark here is buying me a beer!" As they collected their beers and drank deeply, Tony felt a hard push on the shoulder from behind shoving him into the bar and spilling beer onto the front of his shirt. From the corner of his eye he could see Mark stepping back.

Tony didn't move; he was collecting his thoughts as to what he should do next. He saw that Mark was ready to pounce. He then heard a deep, drunken, menacing voice from behind. "Hey, you're Dick's kid, aren't you? He owes me money!"

Tony looked down at the beer on his shirt and over at Mark one more time. "If you've got a problem with the old man, you take it up with him."

The drunk grabbed for Tony's shoulder again and it was the last thing he did before Tony turned and hit him in the face with the pool cue. The pool cue snapped and the shards went flying across the room. As the drunk fell backwards, Tony kicked him in the stomach and drove his fist into what

was left of his face. This brought the room from noisy to
quiet.

The drunk's friends got up from their table and moved
forward, ready for a fight. They only got a few feet before
Skip and the bikers jumped on them and stomped them to
the floor. Mark grabbed Tony and pulled him off the drunk
and tried to get him to cool down. The fight was over quick,
and the drunks realized they were in over their heads. They
collected their unconscious buddy and left the bar.
Everything finally settled down and the guys went back to
their table to take a deep breath and drink some beers. Tony
could see Skip smiling at him from across the table. All
Tony could say was "what?" Skip took a long pull on his
beer, smiled at Tony and said "kinda touchy aren't ya?"

Chapter 16

It takes a certain kind of female to handle the requirements of being a biker's old lady. Oh but there were a few who fit the bill. There were lots that came and went, but the few that stayed were hard core.

Just like each biker had his own personality, so did the women they called their own. It wasn't long after Tony and Mark started spending more time with the club members that this became very obvious.

If you want to know what's tougher than a 200 lb biker, flying down the highway at 105 mph with a rocket between his legs, it's the woman hanging onto him from behind.

Take Kevin's old lady, Marilyn Grant, A.K.A. Zombie. She was the number one lady in the clubhouse and she was always by Kevin's side. She was native, 5'8. She had dark, piercing eyes, always wore large hooped earrings. She had long, straight black hair. She was slender built with some muscle that you didn't notice until she was in a fight. You could see she was tough. She had jailhouse type tattoos, some of them she was tough enough to have done herself. Tony didn't ask.

Her uniform of choice was denim. She carried a knife, hooked on the back of her belt, just in case. She was one of only a few women in the club that was fully patched and they were visible on her denim jacket at all times. She was soft-spoken, direct and articulate, but didn't like to be disrespected. If someone did, she didn't take kindly to it. She had no problem with correcting disrespect physically.

She rode with Kevin and made it known who she belonged to. You could say that she wore his rank and controlled the rest of the girls at all times. She answered to Kevin and she understood that he was the leader.

She got into fights with girls at the bar that she thought were disrespecting her, but she also got into fights with unlucky guys who she might have thought were staring at her too long. For this she would ask if they had gotten an eye-full and then hall off and punch them in face.

Zombie would often voice her displeasure to Kevin about his other attentions to females at the bar. But overall he really just liked seeing her get riled.

Rick's old lady was Patty Smith. She was a little on the heavy side, short blond hair, and blue eyes. She had a lot of piercings in her ears and one in her lip. She constantly swore and she had a hate on for most guys. She wore jeans and high boots. She could ride a bike better than most guys. She came into the club riding her own bike. It was a big Harley that many couldn't handle. She liked to play pool and hated to lose. She kept her eye on Rick because he had a roving eye and frequented the cat house. Rick thought she was great.

She was in a lot of fights at the bar, usually with other women. She assumed that all the girls were after her man and she had to let them know that he was taken. She was very protective of her bike as well and always tried to show her worth. For as long as Tony was in the club she had not received her patch.

She and Zombie had a quiet understanding and they never got in each other's way. But in fights they had each other's backs and they were dangerous.

There were always a number of girls who weren't spoken for by anyone in particular in the clubhouse. They just seemed to ride along with the guys. They partied at the clubhouse and seemed to always be around. Most of these girls would come in for a period of time, a weekend or a month just to check things out and then leave. There were native girls, hookers and girls that came in from other bike clubs, and every now and then, sorority girls.

One of these curious girls was a little French girl named Monique Thibault. She ended up as Skip's girlfriend and became well-entrenched in the club. She liked to fight even though she was five feet nothing. She had red hair, and Skip referred to her as "big boned." He liked them that way. They were an odd couple but they had a lot in common and liked each other. She'd swear at him in French, which he couldn't understand. He'd laugh at her and tell her to speak English "you French bitch." She too was as tough as they came. Monique rode rough shod over the girls who would just come and go. She let them know what they could and couldn't do.

All the girls could hold their own in the drinking category, and when the motorcycle club was in a fight, the girls were more than happy to pitch in.

Chapter 17

Oh yes, there were the sorority girls. A couple of sorority girls had been at a party where a couple of the club members happened to be. Rick was one of these guys and he started talking to the girls. The girls were interested in how they could join this club. Rick was feeding them wild stories about getting them together with the rest of the members so that they could give each other a look and pass an initiation.

There are always a lot of girls at biker parties. They are lured like moths to a flame. Most women, deep down, like at least the idea of being with a "bad boy." The sorority girls were no exception. They were intrigued, but had no idea what a bunch of pot smoking, drinking, dangerous bikers were like.

The guys had a meeting and decided that they would have a "get to know you party" in the near future. This thought brought a chuckle to most of the guys in the club.

None of the club girls would be allowed to attend. This didn't go over well.

A few guys scoped out a farm near Niagara Falls that seemed to be empty. It had a big red barn in a pasture behind the house. They watched the house for a week or two before deciding this would be a great place for the "get to know you" party. It was decided that they would use the barn only and avoid the house at all costs. Obviously there was someone looking after the place and they wanted to avoid a confrontation. This get-together was obviously a gamble.

There were ten sorority girls in all. They ranged in age from about 18 to 20 and had no idea what they were in for. They were going to take these girls out to the barn on this farm to drink and "get to know each other" a little better, and maybe mess around. Everything and everybody was to stay in the barn so as not to create "focus" on the farm.

The barn was a two-storey structure that had a double set of doors on the second level for loading hay into the barn. It was bright red, had a tin roof, and the moldings were painted a bright white. It sat about 100 yards from the house and even though the owners were away, there were still cows in the stalls along one side. The floors were partially concrete and covered with straw. With the cow pens being on one side of the barn, this left plenty of room for the motorcycles on the opposite side. There was electricity in the barn, and once lit up, it was noted that the loft was full of hay bales. Grain bins were attached to the side of the barn.

So the very next weekend, the club members met the sorority girls at the Franklin and invited the girls to ride with them on their bikes. It was obvious they had never been on motorcycles before because they screamed their heads off as they pulled away, as the bikers revved their engines! Tony and Mark had the dubious honour of driving the Chevy van loaded with supplies. Off they went into the night!

They arrived about a half hour later and drove directly into the barn. There was a lot of booze and pot in the van, it was distributed and the party began!

The whole idea, according to the plan, and you know what they say about the best laid plans, was to party out of sight in the barn. The party took place amongst the hay bales and straw on the main level and in the loft.

There is a stark contrast between club member girls and sorority girls. These girls were in way over their heads. Music came from the radios on the bikes; girls were drinking, dancing and asking a lot of questions about the club. Some were sitting on hay bales and others on the members' bikes. Rick was saying that the club wasn't for everyone. The bikers all liked to party hard, but they were in fact a family and protected one another.

The girls weren't innocent, they knew who they were partying with and couples started pairing off, going for walks, etc.

Though Tony was there, he was mainly on the fringe of getting drunk. His lowly position at this party was to serve, but after awhile, the serving part seemed to be over. He found himself on the upper floor of the barn, looking out the swing doors at the farmyard, getting drunker. Eventually, nature called, a piss was needed and Tony just about killed himself trying to get down from the ladder.

Arguments ensued, which more often than not happens when guys, girls and booze are around. Things were heated, but not at the boiling point yet. Outside Tony noticed two guys and girls approaching the house. A couple minutes later the lights went on in the house so it appeared the party had moved!

As time passed, more groups moved to the house, and things were getting really loud with some of the guys gunning their bike engines just in front of the house. Around 2:00 AM noise and activity peaked. Guys were taking some of the girls for rides around the farm yard and the whole party was getting out of hand.

Suddenly in the distance, the dark sky lit up to a stream of red, white and blue lights from police cars coming toward them. Someone had seen the lights on in the farm house and maybe even heard the noise and phoned the police. Cops were coming in from the surrounding areas and swarmed the house and barn. People were scattering, trying to get away on their bikes, although there was only one road in and out.

While all this was happening, Tony was left in the barn, too drunk to move or feel anything. There were a lot of cops moving around the property, looking for bikers and girls.

Mark was trying to get Tony on his feet, but it wasn't happening. According to Mark, Tony had no legs. So Mark dragged Tony into one of the cattle stalls and buried him under hay and cow shit! He then put a pail on his head so that he could breath. Then Mark took off and left him there.

It must have been hours before Tony came too. When he dug himself out of hay and cow shit, the place was empty, no one was around. He felt like he was going to die. At least he smelled like it.

It was just about dawn, as he walked, stumbled, and crawled down the driveway. He sat in the ditch at the side of the road, holding his aching head until he heard a car coming down the road. It was a little green Volkswagen. The car stopped on the road next to him. Mark put his head out the window and said "holy shit man, you're alive!" He had been driving around in a circle around the farm area for about a half hour or so to see if he could find Tony.

Tony got into the car, but he just stunk to high heaven. He was stinking and hung over, as he hung his head out the window and threw up. A few miles down the road they were stopped by a cop that was looking for stragglers from the party. Tony had never looked so bad. It would be impossible to explain this. He had resigned himself to the fact that he was going to jail!

The cruiser that stopped was driven by a veteran police officer of 25 years or more. He believed he had seen and heard everything and couldn't be surprised by anything anymore, until today. He walked up to the car, Mark rolled down the window, and the cop put his head in the car for a better look. That was the wrong thing to do. You could see the old cop's face melt in disbelief at the stench, and the sight of this wretched young man. He knew exactly where the two guys had been! The strongest thing he could say was to call Tony a crazy bastard and to tell Mark to get Tony home!

He walked away from Tony and Mark, shaking his head, knowing that he would never see them again, and truly knowing that he had indeed seen everything.

When the boys got back to the clubhouse; Tony was hosed down in the courtyard and slept in a tent pitched for him.

Some of the guys had been arrested for trespassing. Luckily no one had made the news. Needless to say, none of the sorority girls decided to join the club. Mark told the story of how he had buried Tony in the cow shit and they all laughed like hell, especially when Mark said he put a pail on Tony's head. They continued to laugh like hell and called Tony "a crazy son-of-a-bitch."

The guys told this story everywhere and to anyone who wanted to listen, and how Tony's nickname "crazy" was re-established. Tony wore this nickname like a badge of honour.

Chapter 18

Like most evenings, Tony and Mark were enjoying a cold beer at the Franklin. They talked about the day at work, and how much the Italians were pissing them off. They talked about someday finding another job that would be more worthy of their time and would pay them more money.

As the conversation continued, they noticed the patrons at the table directly behind Mark were having a heated discussion. It eventually led to an all out argument.

Tony and Mark's curiosity was now peaked and they started to listen more closely. There was a bald guy that wore glasses, grey sweatshirt. Tony recognized this guy as a local drug dealer. There was also a heavy set native guy, wearing a plaid shirt and had greasy black hair and a tall thin guy with a long beard wearing a blue jacket. He seemed to be doing most of the talking. Tony and Mark were getting bits and pieces of the conversation as it got louder.

Tall guy says "this really pisses me off." Bald guy says "what the hell are we going to do? Those little bastards are costing us a lot of money and product. How the hell are they finding out where our dealers are? We need to bait them, jump them, and beat the shit out of them! Teach them a lesson!" The greasy-hair guy just seemed to sit there and nod. Tony could see his fists clench, and the rage in his face.

Now Tony and Mark were really interested. They looked at each other wide eyed, eyebrows raised. Someone was going to get an ass-kicking! The heated discussion at the other table continued, with the guys formulating a plan to catch the little bastards. Tall guy says "do we know who they are, where they hang out?" Greasy-hair guy says "Do any of our dealers know who jumped them? Have they given any of you a description?" Bald guy nods, "yeah, one of our dealers told me there were four of the little bastards, one of them was black; he thought he heard one of them call him Sebastian. The other three were white, all around 14. One approached, the other three came in from behind and jumped the dealer. Well you know the rest; they grabbed the money and drugs and buggered off."

Tony and Mark were just about falling off their chairs as they listened. Tony was painfully aware of who these young thugs were, and now, how they would end up. Tony's brother, Ronnie hung out with a bunch of guys, one of them being black and whose name happened to be Sebastian! Not a coincidence! There was nothing else they could do now but listen to the rest of the conversation by the three men.

Bald guy says "I want them, real bad!" Tall guy says "let's set a trap! We'll use some money and drugs as bait and draw them out. When they move on the dealer, we'll jump them and beat the shit out of them! That'll get their attention!" Bald guy says, "We'll set it up for tomorrow night." Tall guy agrees; greasy hair guy nods.

Tony and Mark look at one another and motion toward the bar. They got up slowly so as not to cause attention and moved toward the bar. Sitting down, they ordered a beer and a shot. Tony looked Mark right in the eye and said "that's my asshole kid brother they're talking about! I haven't seen him in quite a while, but I know that's him." Mark took a long pull on his beer, looked down at the shot glass and said "what do you want to do about it? Whatever it is, I'm with you!"

Tony and Mark knew they didn't have much time. They'd use the Chevy van and go and find Ronnie the next day. Tony knew that Ronnie didn't spend a whole lot of time at home but knew some of the places he liked to hang out at with his buddies. He knew that Ronnie wouldn't be at school, he'd quit after grade six.

Tony and Mark skipped work and grabbed the van next morning and went hunting for Ronnie. They drove around for some time and were just about ready to give up, when they saw him come out of John's Pool Hall with his buddy Sebastian. Tony and Mark watched them as they walked up the street. Tony and Mark drove up to them and as they got closer, Mark rolled down the window and yelled "hey you bastards, we want to talk to you!" At that very moment Ronnie and Sebastian split up and ran in different directions.

Ronnie eventually turned into an alley that turned out to be a dead end! Tony and Mark used the van to block the alley. They got out of the van and walked into the alley and caught up to him and grabbed him by the coat. Up until now, Ronnie was unaware of who was chasing him, until they spun him around and pushed him up against the wall. Fear and recognition set in all at once. Ronnie realized it was Tony and Mark. Ronnie was not happy to see his brother, and less happy to be pushed up against a wall.

Tony told Ronnie that he was not impressed to have to come and find him, and that he was in deep shit. He also told him that he knew about what he had been doing with his buddies, and other people did too. Tony explained to Ronnie what he had overheard and that he was about to get his ass kicked!

With that, Tony and Mark threw Ronnie in the van. They tried to explain to him what would happen if he continued his escapades and the trap that was set for him and his buddies that night. These were dangerous people he was ripping off and they wouldn't put up with it anymore. They then drove to the old man's house.

It wasn't a long ride, but it sure was a quiet one. Ronnie wasn't saying a word. He'd just head out again as soon as Tony left.

When they got to the house, they opened the van door, grabbed Ronnie by the collar and marched him up to the front door. Tony didn't bother knocking, just went right in.

Familiar sights and smells assaulted their senses. Tony could smell stale cigarette smoke and what he thought to be that of a backed-up bathroom. From the front door Tony could see into the kitchen. There at the table his mother sat, hunched over a half finished beer, cigarette hanging from her mouth. Tony was pretty sure she wasn't even aware that he was there. There were dishes overflowing in the sink, and more on the table.

Tony's attention was directed to the living room where his old man was sitting in his favourite chair in front of the TV, the exact spot he sat last time Tony saw him. He was wearing the same clothes too, a dirty pair of sweatpants, and an old wife beater t-shirt. Tony led Ronnie towards him and let him go. Ronnie continued through the living room towards his bedroom. Before he got there he turned around and told Tony to "fuck off you bastard." He continued to his room and slammed the door.

The old man hadn't moved or even raised his eyes. He didn't even acknowledge that Tony was there. Tony's eyes burned into the old man as he moved towards the chair. He wasn't sure if he was going to hit him, he was that mad. Instead, he took a deep breath, looked squarely at him and said "I see you're still not doing your job!" With that, he turned around and walked out of the house, Mark trailing closely behind. Tony thought that he did all he really could have done.

Tony wasn't sure if Ronnie had gotten the message or not. He never saw the three men at the Franklin again; and never heard of anything going down. Ten days later Tony heard, through the grapevine, that Ronnie and Sebastian had stepped up their game and stole a car. They were caught quickly when they crashed into another car. Last he heard they were both on their way to Reform School. It was a hard lesson to learn; he hoped they'd learn it.

Chapter 19

The guys from the club were accepting Tony and Mark more and more. They were getting invited to other bars that the club members hung out at; and they also found themselves participating in some of the scraps that the guys got into. It was an unconventional comradery allowing the boys to feel accepted, safe, and a part of something.

One of the ways they knew they were being accepted was that Skip gave them tasks from time to time. One of Tony's new tasks was as lookout while the club members were "acquiring" items from parked trucks or warehouses that were unattended. He wasn't privy to everything that was going on, but he had a feeling that he was earning a trust and being let in a bit at a time. They understood that Tony had their backs and it was a lead-in to one day becoming a club member. Tony found that there were a lot of "little bits" to being fully let in.

Most of the discussions that occurred when Tony and Mark got together with the club members involved bikes and broads. They of course spoke about the boys' escapades, the fights they had had, and of course the race. But this evening Skip spoke more directly to Tony.

He started asking Tony a lot of questions about his family and had he been in trouble with the law. This made Tony uneasy because he didn't like discussing the situation he had just left.

He wanted to know what Tony was getting from hanging with the club, since he had been around now for quite some time. He was also asked what he wanted from the club. Tony said that he wanted to become a member, but wasn't sure if he had all that it would take. It was also important to Tony to know if anyone had any beefs with him during his time with the club. He didn't get any opposition from the guys sitting at the table, but he did get a lot of good feedback. There was one shot that Skip had received from Zombie. She said that he was too skinny, but she also said that he could hold his own, so it was ok.

Tony and Mark mentioned that they would be going into the club the next day, when Skip interrupted them and told them they had to stay away for about a week because of club business, but he did mention that they were welcome to the van if they needed it. The boys didn't know what was going on, but they weren't privy to the club's business dealings and apparently right now it was "member's only"; they'd have to busy themselves elsewhere.

Tony and Mark hung out at the Franklin all week when they weren't working. They were still crashing at Mark's house and going there for a change of clothes and sometimes Olive would have something for the boys to eat. A few days after they were told not to go to the club house, Mark and Tony finished their shift at the winery and headed to Mark's house to change. As they came up on the house, an ambulance was just driving away, and there was a police car out front. Then they saw a cop, dragging Shamus out in handcuffs and putting him in the backseat of the patrol car. Many of the neighbours were on the sidewalk, and Mark stopped one to ask what the hell was happening.

The neighbour told Mark that they heard a loud shouting match, which wasn't unusual but then there was a loud crashing noise and a scream which made them call the cops.

Mark and Tony rushed to the hospital to find out that Olive had a concussion from being slammed into the wall. She also had bruises and scratches on her arms. She would be fine, but needed to stay in the hospital overnight for observation due to the concussion.

Mark vowed that Olive would not be returning to the house. He was going to find her and his siblings some other place to live. One of Mark's sisters had gotten married and there were still three siblings living at home.

The boys went in to see Olive and were witness to the state she was in. She told Mark about Shamus coming home in a drunken rage and there was no calming him down. She told Mark that she would not press charges against her husband, but was more than happy to have him spend some time in jail before she let them know her wishes.

The next morning, Mark and Tony borrowed the van and went to Olive's house to gather belongings. They also took the rest of their stuff as well. It was decided that Mark's sisters would live with their married sister. As luck would have it, they found a small place for Olive and Billy in the projects, safe from Shamus. As soon as Olive was released, they picked her up from the hospital and Olive let the cops know that she was not pressing charges. The cops informed her that they would be releasing him.

After settling Olive into her new surroundings, Mark and Tony headed back to the house to await Shamus.

They didn't have to wait long. A cruiser pulled up in front of the house and let Shamus out of the back seat. He was in definite need of a shave and he looked like a bag of shit.

Mark watched him as he came up the walk to the front door and stepped inside. Shamus walked through the door but wasn't ready for the rage on the other side. Mark grabbed him by the shirt and slammed him up against the wall, cracking the drywall. He didn't wait for Shamus to respond, he slammed his knee into his testicles and as he went down Mark pummeled him while yelling at him "you bastard."

Tony watched while this was happening, but he could tell when Mark's anger turned from rage to something darker. It was time to end it. Shamus had had enough. Tony put his arm around Mark's neck and pulled him off. It was all he could do to keep Mark away from him. Tony told Mark it was time to leave and pulled him toward the door. Mark sensed that Tony was right but as he left he screamed "if you ever touch my mother again, I'll kill you! You're lucky Skip is out of town, or you'd be dead already! Remember though, he will be coming back!"

With business done with, and Olive, safely tucked away and resting, Mark and Tony drove over to the Franklin with the van. They pulled into the parking lot at the Franklin and Tony said "I really need a beer." Mark looked at Tony and said "you go ahead, I've got something I've got to do; I'll get back to you." He then left Tony in the parking lot and drove away.

Tony took a few deep breaths and entered the back door to the Franklin and went straight to the bar. He asked Mo for a beer and started to go over the events of the last 24 hours. He also wondered where the hell they were going to live.

Mo watched him from the other side of the bar. It was the first time he'd seen Tony come into the bar on his own. Mo sauntered up to him and leaned over the bar toward Tony. "Why the long face?" Tony found himself telling Mo what had happened in the last 24 hours. He told him about the fight and how the boys were now homeless. Mo thought about it for a bit, sighed, and decided to tell Tony that he might have an idea.

Mo was living in a rooming house down near the lake and as fate would have it, he knew that a room had become available. He knew the lady that ran the place. Liz kept a clean establishment and provided some hot meals. She also provided comfort for Mo on some cold lonely nights. At that thought Mo smiled to himself. He also knew he would be able to vouch for Tony and Mark and was sure she would be able to help them.

Mo then let Tony know about his plan. Tony couldn't believe his luck and was looking forward to letting Mark know. They could easily bunk together if they needed to! Life was good.

Tony was excited at the prospect of actually having his own place. Before he finished his second beer, he looked up to see Mark strolling into the bar. He noticed a calmness about him that wasn't there earlier and he also noticed that his damaged hand was bandaged.

Tony usually respected Mark's privacy but this time he had to know where his friend had been. Mark came over and sat at the stool next to Tony and ordered a beer. Tony said "well?" Mark took a deep breath and told Tony that he was at Christine's house. Tony then said "who the hell is Christine?" Mark told Tony that Christine was his girlfriend and that he had been spending more and more time with her lately. Suddenly a light came on and Tony then realized why he had been missing of late, sometimes for a couple of hours and sometimes overnight!

Mark said he needed to tell Christine what had happened and when he did Christine suggested he move in with her. Mark told Tony that he was sorry that it would put him in a bind, but he needed to do this. Tony then broke out in thunderous laughter and said "really?" Mark was confused at what just happened with his friend, he never expected laughter. Then Tony told him about Mo's offer.

They both started laughing; things were going to work out just fine.

Mo called Liz to let her know she had a new tenant and Tony followed Mo to the rooming house after closing. Liz was in the kitchen waiting to meet Tony and show him the room.

She was average height and curvy. She had strawberry blond hair that she wore on top of her head. Glasses dangled from a chain around her neck and her lips were painted red. She reminded Tony of "Miss Kitty" on "Gunsmoke". After shaking Tony's hand, she led him upstairs to the room that would be his.

The room wasn't large or fancy but it was his and he loved it! It had a large bed on the back wall made up with large pillows and a homemade quilt. There was a night stand beside the bed with a lamp. There was a dresser with a small TV and a small table next to the window overlooking the boardwalk.

All in all it had been a busy week. A couple days later, while at the Franklin, Skip and some of the guys came in and sat down with Tony and Mark. Mark let Skip know what had transpired at their old man's house and how Mark looked after things. He also told him where Olive was now living.

Skip was impressed with the way Mark had handled things and said he probably would have done the same.

While they were sitting there, conversation turned to the clubhouse and Skip looked at the guys and told them that they could come back to the clubhouse the next evening; the club business was over.

Chapter 20

They did indeed return to the clubhouse the next evening as they were told. They didn't expect anything unusual. They also didn't expect the whole chapter being there; this amounted to about 65 guys. There were no questions asked about the boys being there. Tony had been in fights with them and alongside them. Everyone was milling around, drinking beer. Satan was in fine form as he gave everyone a tongue lashing.

Kevin then stood up and this brought about quiet. He talked about club business and the fact that they were thinking about bringing in some new members. John Butler and Fred Cummings, a couple of Lone Wolf riders, had stripped their patches and were asking to become members of Lucifer's Army. This was one of the topics that had been discussed in the week prior.

The two Lone Wolves were there. Kevin asked them to stand up and tell the group about themselves. He then asked the membership if anyone had any bitches with these two, in terms of money, drugs or if they could be trusted. No one said anything at this point and the two sat down. Kevin said "all in favour of letting these two ex-Lone Wolves into the Army on a probationary period; say Aye." The room reverberated with a resounding "Aye." There were no "nays". He then slammed a beer bottle on the table and said "the Ayes have it."

He asked if anyone would stand for them or sponsor them. Two of the Army members stood up and said they'd be responsible for them. Pete and Floyd Flynn, brothers and long-standing members of the Army were to be the ex-Wolf sponsors. They were probably going to be watched closer than anyone, since they all knew that because they were ex-Lone Wolves; they could be spies.

Tony and Mark were taking all of this in and couldn't believe what was happening in front of their eyes. Why were they there? This was club business.

There was an Indian guy and a black guy from the states. They were really mean-looking. Kevin asked them to stand and then asked the group if anyone had any beefs or dealings with them. He went on and finally asked would anyone stand for them. Four Army members said they would stand for them.

Tony was fascinated. He hadn't seen anything like this before in his life.

Then Skip came over to Mark and Tony and asked them to stand up. Tony wasn't sure what the hell was going on. He was anxious, excited and scared all at once. Skip started to talk to Kevin and the group and asked to have the group vote on them.

Kevin didn't say anything. Skip went around asking different members if they had any dealings with them, knew them, or if they thought they had club potential.

Tony was frozen and didn't know what to say, as he watched Skip work the room asking questions about them to the members. Skip was telling Kevin and the members about the fact that they were local boys, growing up in the neighbourhood, and the fact that they were loyal and could be trusted. Then everything went quiet, and Tony had the worst case of dry mouth he had ever had.

Skip went over to Kevin and talked for a long time. Then Kevin stood up and asked everyone in the room if they had any bitches with these two guys and did they owe anyone anything? Someone in the back yelled "aren't you that bastard that got buried in the cow shit?" Everyone in the room howled! Kevin hammered his beer on the table for a third time that evening. He said they were on probation as

Prospects until he said otherwise. They were to keep their noses clean, and if anyone in the club, at any time asked them to do something, they were to do it right away, and with no questions. He said again "anytime, anywhere. If they screwed up in the probationary period, they were gone!"

One of the guys Tony had been riding with occasionally, Ken Manning piped up and said that he wasn't going to allow Tony's ass on his bike anymore! He told Tony he had to get his own bike and learn how to ride, because he wouldn't be carting him around anymore. This brought more laughter.

With business completed everyone relaxed and got drunk while Tony started his Prospect duties tending the bar for the rest of the night.

Chapter 21

Getting your own bike doesn't happen overnight, so the boys continued driving the van and being gophers. They picked up parts, made deliveries, picked up guys who had broken down, made booze runs, and made deliveries to the warehouse. They tended bar, cleaned up every night after the parties, picked up girls and dropped them off the next day. Sometimes they even had to get the girls from the cathouse to outside appointments and deliver them back. There was always food that needed to be bought, but thankfully Tony and Mark never had to cook it; that would have been a mistake. Being a Prospect was anything but dull, and along with these duties the boys also had their jobs at the winery.

For some time, this was enough to be content. Mark also had the dubious honour of polishing some of the club member's bikes. They had to shine like glass, or he'd be doing it over again. Tony was happy that this task was not given to him, at least not yet. Tending to 30 or 40 guys keeps a body busy. In effect they did what a "girl Friday" would do. This meant that they did anything and everything.

The work needed to be done, but it was a way for the club members to see how much Tony and Mark could take. They were constantly testing for weakness. Tony never had a problem with this. He used it as a dipstick to see where he could improve and become more valuable. These things weren't confrontational, but they were put into situations to see how they'd react.

At the same time all this was going on, they were also being taught about the club, and what was expected as a club member. One guy said that the best way to get out of the probation phase was just to shut up and listen. Tony and Mark were the youngest members that were brought into the club at only 18. Most members came with a hardness already built in and life lessons learned. The boys were being tended to slowly.

There was a lot to learn in the club and Tony and Mark were learning all the rules and how to live by them. Never back down, never surrender, never show fear and your brothers at arms were your brothers. These were beat into the boys every day in different ways. If one of your brothers gets too drunk, and his mouth gets him into trouble, you step in. Doesn't matter if he was right or wrong, the club came first and nothing else.

Every day someone reminded Mark and Tony that they didn't have a bike. It was after all, a bike club. This was embarrassing and painful to listen to. Tony felt this especially when the club would go on a "run". To Tony this was a show of force. They might be travelling close to the territory of a rival club. The gang members would head out on their bikes, riding out of the compound one after another. Then at the very end, there was Tony and Mark driving out of the compound in their small van, with all the supplies that were required for partying. They wanted to be actual members and all that that entailed. They worked their asses off trying to do everything that was asked. But they also had to have initiative in order to make things happen for themselves.

Mark and Tony spent a lot of time in that stupid little van.

During one of these outings they went to the Department of Motor Vehicles and got a handbook so they could study and pass the test for riding a motorcycle. They spent hours upon hours in the van asking each other questions from the handbook. They didn't tell anyone that they were doing this because, really, they probably would have all laughed at them. It probably would have been considered wimpy.

When they thought they were ready, they went to the DMV dressed as "ordinary citizens." They wanted to make a good impression and didn't feel comfortable going in as a couple of "biker wannabes." That probably wouldn't have helped their cause. They had on brand new jeans, runners and sweatshirts, windbreakers and ball caps. They sat in the DMV with everyone else that was writing their motorcycle tests.

Wouldn't you know it! They aced it! The lady at the window handed them their learner licenses, stamped them and told them to go and celebrate! So they went out and had a couple of beers. This brought on another problem. They still didn't have bikes. How the hell were they going to take their tests? Without bikes they couldn't practice and pass the practical test! This was kind of a big deal.

They really hadn't thought about this much until then. They were sitting in the clubhouse in the middle of the week, not sure what they were going to do about their transportation problem. Skip and a couple of other guys came in and saw them at the table. Skip came over and sat down. He looked them right in the eye and asked "so do you know how to ride?"

The boys looked at each other and back at Skip. It seemed like forever before they could answer. No one had bothered to ask them before. Skip knew what the answer was of course because Mark was Skip's brother. If Mark had been riding, Skip would know. He knew what the answer was, but he wanted to hear it from them anyway.

They both said "no" in unison. It wasn't a planned event. They both had lumps in their throats when they answered. They confessed to him that they had been studying and had gone to the DMV and gotten their learner's permits. Skip continued to look at them hard. At that point, Mark and Tony felt like boys again. All of a sudden, Skip laughed his ass off.

After a bit, he stopped laughing. He looked at Mark and smiled. Something he never did. Tony thought he was looking at Mark, not like the Sergeant at Arms of a bike club, not like a club member responsible for him, but like a brother. Tony had never witnessed this before.

Skip got up, leaned over the table with his two hands planted. He looked at Mark and then at Tony and said "ok, we're going to do this right." They didn't know what he meant at the time, but they were eager, anxious and scared to find out. Skip then walked away from the table to where the other club members were seated.

Mark and Tony looked at each other in amazement and disbelief. "What was that and what now?"

For the next few days, nothing else happened. Everything seemed to be "regular." Regular club business, regular club runs.

Tony and Mark had just come back from Niagara Falls, where they had picked up some motorcycle parts. They drove into the yard and then into the compound. There were a bunch of guys down there and a bunch of bikes.

Rick and Skip were talking to the guys. Like good Prospects, they went over to them and Rick and Skip turned around to acknowledge them. Rick asked them how they were doing. He said that he heard that they had gotten their learner's permits. This immediately brought chuckles from the whole group.

Rick said if they were going to be in this club and learn how to ride motorcycles, they were going to learn everything about motorcycles, not just how to ride. He had been talking to about four or five of the other guys who had volunteered to teach Tony and Mark everything about motorcycles and how to ride.

Tony was awestruck. A couple of guys came over to help them. They said that by the time they were done, the two of them would know everything there was to know about riding, and they wouldn't let them take the test until they were sure Mark and Tony were ready.

Tony thought this meant that they would be doing maintenance on the Harleys. He thought they would be stripping and modifying and of course riding a big badass Harley. This was pretty heady. Tony's mind was racing a mile a minute. Tony could just see himself working on these club bikes, hundreds of thousands of dollars worth of engines in their hands. He was pretty happy at the prospect.

He could see Mark's jaw was hanging wide open. He looked around to see everybody talking at once and making plans. Mark and Tony walked among the bikes with a new prospective. They were told they would know everything there was to know, and if they didn't, they'd beat their asses! They could smell the rubber and the power that these machines gave off.

Tony was waiting for someone to say "you're going to work on this bike, and I'll watch you." This would mean that they truly trusted Mark and Tony with their rides. Reality was about to set in.

Skip then directed them over to the far corner of the workshop and there, they noticed a couple of bikes. Not at all like the others. Even they could see they were pieces of shit. There was a Honda 500, not a Harley. It was orange, black and rusty. Next to it was a shitty black Yamaha. The Honda had a standard flat seat and the leather was cracked and sun burned. The tires on both bikes were flat, spokes were rusted and the shocks were gone. The Yamaha was covered in oil and dirt. The boys were deflated.

They were hoping against hope that this was not what they had in mind for the boys. They weren't saying anything, but both Mark and Tony had the same sinking deflated feeling.

Skip came up to them, slapped them on their backs and said "these are your babies. You two guys are each going to have one of these." He said the club members were going to teach them how to tear the bikes down and build them back up again, even better. They'd better do a good job, because these were the bikes they were going to do their tests on.

Mark piped up "on this piece of shit?" Rick said "yeah, it is! But it's your piece of shit!" And they were also required to pay the club $200 each for them. You don't get anything for nothing!

It took them weeks to strip the bikes down. They still had regular club duties and work. So they did it in their spare time, anytime they could manage, they would work on their bikes.

They thought their bikes were pigs. Everything was rusted, soiled or broken. Mark and Tony thought they must have been found in a junkyard and brought back as a joke.

There was always someone around when they were working on their bikes. It wasn't planned, as far as they knew; it just happened that way. The machine shop at the club was built for motorcycle repair, and it was amazing. There was nothing lacking. The guys who taught them never laid a finger on the bikes or tools. It was their bikes and no one would touch them, but the boys.

They took the engines out and sand-blasted the frames. They found that the Honda engine had seized and Mark's piston had gone through the head at some point. It was determined, at that time, that the engines weren't coming back to life, and they'd need replacements.

Three days later, just like Christmas, beside the bikes were new, rebuilt engines. No one said anything, it really was Christmas. They still had to take them apart, so that they could compare them to the old ones and see why they weren't working.

They remounted them in the sand-blasted, newly painted frames. This was about five weeks after they started the projects. Anything they couldn't sand down and repair was replaced. Funny, parts just happen to come in. Mark and Tony didn't ask questions, because they knew.

In the end, they looked like pretty good pieces of shit. Now they had to learn to ride.

Chapter 22

Starting a bike is easy; you put the key in and turn. As long as you have gas in the tank, it will start; then comes the hard part. All bikes have manual transmissions, so you have to learn how to shift. They had driven standard cars before but shifting a bike is different. The hardest part about shifting on a bike is the hand clutch. The bike won't move unless the clutch is engaged. If you let it out too fast, the front of the bike will jump up in the air and put you on your ass.

When learning to ride they were told to start in second gear, rather than first. The bike reacts slower, and will move without stalling out. There was a lot of practicing up and down the length of the compound. As always, there were a couple of guys there teaching. "Remember to put your feet down, only after it stops!" The secret, through trial and error, was to keep your feet on the pegs, no matter what. It's all a matter of practice, going straight and turning because of course, when you're turning, you have to lean into the turn.

A Honda 500 is a small bike, but it is very powerful. You have to learn how to go fast, but you also have to learn how to go very slow. There is a knack to both. Balance is always an integral part. There is an art to balancing the bike when it is barely moving. From there, you learn how to turn. This is a combination of balance and speed. Never put your foot down!

They practiced every day, up and down the compound. The guys would constantly remind them to relax, don't stiffen up and enjoy the ride. Tony kept getting into shit for using his front brake before applying the back; doing this can throw you over the handlebars, which luckily didn't happen; but his ass lifted up off his seat a few times giving him enough of a scare.

After some time, they moved the lessons to a big shopping centre parking lot. They practiced serpentines, which are very large S's. This got them used to getting into turns at slow speed. After a few days, they played follow the leader with one of the club members. They had to do everything the leader would do. Speeding up and slowing down real fast, using the back brake first, practice, lots of practice.

It eventually felt like the bikes became part of them. They knew they were ready to go for their tests. Tony and Mark knew without a doubt that they could pass the test. The guys in the club were really good teachers. There wasn't anything they hadn't tried a hundred times.

They made appointments on the weekend so that everyone was around. So on an early Saturday morning the guys headed out on the Honda and Yamaha, again wearing their windbreakers and helmets. They were followed by three of the club members.

The test was in two parts, one was in the parking lot and the other was on the road. Skip stayed with the other two club members on the far side of the parking lot. There were about 10 guys taking the test. Tony and Mark knew that there were a few things that would bring about an immediate fail. Taking your feet off the pegs was one of them.

There were three instructors and they had set out a track made of traffic cones. The idea of the cones was so that you have to turn your bike left or right around them, very slowly. This would make it clear to the instructors if you had control of the bike. They made you go through, what amounted to a serpentine and at the end you were to make a sweeping turn facing one of the instructors, gunning your engine and racing towards him. There was a line drawn in front of him, and that's where you had to stop, right on the line. If you missed the line, or stopped without control, you failed.

There are a lot of ways to fail, but the boys were trained correctly.

After everyone had gone through the course and passed, they were told that they were going out into the street in a group and drive around town. Tony and Mark thought this was going to be cool.

They put one instructor in front and one behind. They all pulled out of the parking lot. Skip and the two other club members followed the gaggle of newbie bikers and their instructors.

They had driven around for about 15 minutes, just coming off Ontario Street and all of a sudden they heard big motorcycles. Tony didn't know until after that Skip and some of the club members, at least four, came up on the road course and tucked in behind the rear instructor to follow the parade of new bikers. Tony and Mark thought this was great; but this unnerved the instructors.

The test lasted about a half an hour. They then found themselves back in the DMV parking Lot. Skip and the other club members hung out at the end of the lot. All of the new bikers went into the DMV where they were told officially that they had all passed. As soon as Tony and Mark received their stamps, they ran out to their bikes and met up with Skip and the other bikers at the end of the lot.

They told Skip and the guys that they were good as gold. At that, Skip pulled out their leather Prospect Cuts, followed by slaps on the back of their helmets. One of the guys said "let's get the hell out of here!"

They did a victory lap around town and then went back to the clubhouse. They parked their bikes downstairs and commenced to party the rest of the weekend. It was a really good time. Something the boys would never forget.

Chapter 23

With each of these steps, the boys felt more and more accepted as part of the bike gang.

After the celebration of the boys receiving their motorcycle licenses, it was again "business as usual." The boys went back to the things they normally did as Prospects, while still working at the winery. The difference was that when they had free time, they could go for a ride on their little shit bikes. While this was a step up from the van, they were definitely not chick magnets.

Tony and Mark continued to stay close together. They genuinely liked each other. They felt they could support or protect each other in whatever way was needed. They spent a lot of time talking to the other members about their bikes because, of course, Mark and Tony were fascinated and in the near future wanted to ride Harleys as well.

At this point Mark and Tony were still pretty naïve about where the club got most of their money. They knew that they boosted transports for their cargo and broke into warehouses and sold this material on the black market. They were privy to the warehouse where the guys stored the items they acquired. They knew that drugs were getting more prevalent, allowing for easy money to be made. However, they knew there had to be more.

Mark and Tony were still working at the winery, bringing home a pittance. It kept them eating, paying rent and beer, but nothing was left to scrape together money needed for a decent ride.

They decided to speak to Skip and Rick about possibly making more money. Rick said that it was always possible to become more "involved" in order to earn cash. Tony and Mark didn't realize it at the time, but this was just the way the bikers dragged new guys deeper into the club.

Rick told them they could make money on a couple of projects in the warehouse district down by the docks. It ended up that Tony and Mark, set off with Skip and stole a couple of transport trucks full of electronic equipment. They found out later that the club had someone working for them on the inside of the transport company that would let the gang know when shipments were coming in that carried desirable items. He would also give the Army the routes so that the trucks could be hi-jacked before they reached the warehouse.

They took the stolen trucks and drove them into the Mississauga warehouse district. This is where the Army's warehouse was located. They offloaded them into the warehouse to be sold at a later date.

While they were there, they couldn't help but stand in awe of all the stuff piled there. Once they were done, they took the transports out and abandoned them.

Skip had been following them, making sure there was no trouble, picking them up after and taking them back to the club house.

Tony and Mark made $3000 each that night. When they found out how easy it was to make money, real money, they quit the winery. It was at this time that Tony could make his first down payment on his new ride.

Chapter 24

Tony and Mark were performing their "Prospect" duties at the club one hot summer's evening. Beers were flowing like water and Tony had gone to the back storage area to get fresh bottles of booze for the bar. It was going to be a long night. As he returned and was coming around the corner carrying two flats of beer, he became aware of a commotion going on around the bar area. Satan was giving everyone hell.

When he entered the room, he could see that some "visitors" had arrived. There were about six of them, bikers for sure, from another club. He had not seen the patch before, but no one was getting upset, so he guessed that it was alright. Then he noticed something else. One of them was female.

Tony moved to the back of the bar and observed a lot of handshaking and back slapping. The girl even gave Junior a big hug! Junior was a very large man, and that wasn't an easy thing to do. He was a ranking member in the club, full patch and liked by everyone.

Tony busied himself behind the bar; replenishing empty bottles and then took the empties to the back of the building to get rid of them. When he returned Mark had brought beers and plates of food out to the travelers.

Once Tony finished his duties he had the time to focus on what was going on. He couldn't take his eyes off her. She wasn't like any of the other girls that belonged in Lucifer's Army. All of them were way too thorny, tough looking and the things they spewed from their mouths would make a sailor blush.

This girl was different, she was about medium height, maybe 5'5, and this Tony guessed when she stood beside Junior who was 6'6. She wore jeans that fit her really well, boots, jean shirt and she wore her black hair in a long braid down her back. She had high cheek bones. In fact Tony thought of her as being "pretty," sitting there. She was a stark contrast to the bikers she was sitting with.

Sometime later Tony decided that he could use some air. He stepped out onto the front porch. By this time, the streets were quieting and it was dark. It was a clear cool night, and he took a deep breath. As he was taking in the night air, he heard the door behind him. He turned and there she was!

She said seriously, her eyes sparkling, "you were staring at me. Am I familiar to you?" Tony didn't know what to say, at that moment he couldn't speak. She then said her name was Betty Ladoux. Tony could then hear himself tell her his name. She then asked Tony if there was somewhere quiet, out of the noise, where she could go.

Tony could only think of one place—the van. He motioned to her to follow him and she did. When they arrived at the van, Tony spread a few blankets down on the floor. They were kept in the van for covering contraband. Once he was finished and about to walk away, Betty sat down and motioned to Tony to join her. Up until then he thought she wanted the place just to rest, away from everyone. He did sit down and Betty offered him a beer, which he hadn't noticed she had. She took a drink of hers and Tony took a long drink down his very dry throat.

She was even prettier up close in the dim light. Tony figured she was just a bit older than he. She told him that her brother belonged to the bike club for years and that he had raised her in amongst the club since she was very young and their parents had died. They had been good to her and had protected her, but she belonged to no one. She had just come along for the ride. They had been to Montreal and were on

their way back to the states when they thought they would
stop to see friends and her distant cousin, Junior.

Tony didn't say much about himself, he didn't feel there
was much to say anyway. But he really enjoyed listening to
her.

They had nearly finished their beers when he glanced at
her and noticed a look that was familiar to him. He wasn't
totally inexperienced. There was that one time with a senior
in the school basement that had been quick and heated, no
emotion. Since then, there'd been a couple of others,
connections he made while not in a sober state of mind.

Betty grabbed Tony's shirt and pulled him close for
what Tony thought was a mind blowing kiss. This wasn't at
all like his first experience. The kiss was slow, and felt warm
and real and led to something Tony had never experienced
before, passion. After, she actually let Tony put his arm
around her and soon they fell asleep.

Tony woke at dawn to the sound of revving motorcycle
engines. He looked out to see that the visitors were mounted
on their Harleys and with one more gun of their engines,
they drove off.

It might have been his imagination, but before they
drove away Tony thought he saw Betty look over at the van

and smile. Then they were gone. He thought he would never see her again, but he would never forget her.

Tony tidied up the van and headed to the clubhouse just in time to see Junior coming out the door. He stopped Tony in his tracks, looked down at him and said "you better have treated her right boy." He looked Tony in the eye and the look spoke volumes. Junior then turned and went back into the clubhouse followed by Tony. Junior turned once more and put his hand on Tony's shoulder and said "my bike needs to be cleaned and shined Prospect, get to it."

Mark was already in the clubhouse cleaning up. As Tony approached the bar, he looked up and said "where the hell have you been?"

Chapter 25

It was just a frame and a set of forks to start. It cost Tony $1200. Skip and the other guys said there would be no problem getting parts. This was true for Mark as well. Sometimes it cost them a bit of money, but most of the time it did not.

It was a fascinating time. They were actually building real Harleys! They had money in their pockets, and there seemed to be a rhythm. Without even thinking about it, they were again being sucked in deeper into the motorcycle gang. Mark understood this right away, and didn't have any problem with it. It took Tony longer to understand, but he could see the way it was going. For the time being he was content with his role and the perks he got kept his mind occupied. There was easy money to be made and the boys took advantage of it. They also got into a lot of fights. Some Tony created himself, just by being an asshole. A lot of times they were back up for the other members who got into fights with guys who challenged the gang.

The club was making a lot of money. They were more and more into everything; stolen merchandise, drugs, girls and extortion. More and more guns were entering into the picture. If you were a biker, things were good. Ordinary people were afraid of you, and they pretty much all felt that this was a good thing.

Tony and Mark's bikes were coming along. Tony had to straighten his frame, but it came around easily. The engine came in and Tony paid $500 for it, which was a tenth of what it was really worth. All the parts came in on a regular basis. Tony was more on his own now, as he became more and more involved with the gang.

Mark was still there, but Tony did more on his own. There were more drugs, more girls. Tony was now carrying a gun. The club's business was getting really big, and there were more members being added to their ranks. Now that Tony and Mark had their own "shit bikes" and the build on their Harleys was coming along, it was up to other "Prospects" to take on the "van duties." This included deliveries to the warehouse.

The club was not only doing business in Toronto, but also Niagara Falls and across the border into the states.

It took Tony the rest of the winter and into the spring to get his Harley together. She sure was pretty when she was done. She was painted dark, dark blue, 1963 Harley Sportster, 880 cc with an engine rated out to 1000cc. She was a rocket with a short fuse. Top speed was 115 – 125 mph with a weight of 540 lbs. Tony was barely 180 lbs, so there was little weight to slow her down.

Mark built a Harley Shovel Head, 1000cc, jet black, like his brother, Skip's. It had an oversized tire on the back and made an evil sound, more like a growl when it moved. Tony drove his bike enumerable hours, all over the province.

Tony and Mark thought they had it made, they always talked about how lucky they were. Tony especially thought he had the world by the ass, after coming from his early life. Sometime later, Tony would realize how really untrue this was.

Chapter 26

Once the Harleys were running beautifully, a celebration was in order. The boys decided to take them on a run. Not a long one, two to three days. The club wouldn't miss them. There were now plenty of "Prospects" to go around.

They talked about where they should go. Neither wanted to go to Montreal and the biker Mecca of Sturgis would be just too far right now. The boys each mentally put the trip to Sturgis on a to-do list.

They then thought of going south and discussed possible destinations. Mark happened to say "too bad we don't know anyone down there." Tony was thoughtful for a few minutes, and then said "well, I guess I sort of do." A warm feeling came across him. He remembered a kiss and a fondness, Betty came to mind. Mark could see the look crossing his face and said "you're shitting me, the girl? You wanna go see the girl?" Tony smiled, "maybe," it is a place we could go. Mark shook his head, and was walking away, muttering to himself "I've never been to Pennsylvania." This was the home of the Harpy's Motorcycle Gang that Betty's brother belonged to.

The boys were trying to find a way to talk to Skip about leaving for a couple of days on a road trip to break the bikes in. As luck would have it, Kevin's bike was in dire need of a special carburetor that they were having trouble finding. He had put the word out and a day or so later, word came back from an associate motorcycle club that they had such a part. Junior was related to one of the members and they had been both friends and business associates with the club for some time. They would need someone to go down to Springfield Pennsylvania to meet up with the club and pick up the part as soon as possible.

Skip already knew that Tony and Mark wanted to go on a run; this would be the perfect time to get this out of their system and retrieve the part that was so badly needed. Skip saw it as a win/win. He ran it past Rick and got the go ahead.

It was a wise move that all club members, including Prospects had passports. This was done because they were so close to the border that it wasn't unusual for members to go back and forth.

When Skip broke the news to the guys that they were cleared to go, their faces broke out in big shit eating grins at the prospect of getting away. Skip told them they would be leaving early next morning for Springfield, Pennsylvania. They were to go to the Harpy's clubhouse and ask for Pierre Ladoux. They were told they couldn't miss him.

Pierre Ladoux was the Sergeant at Arms for the club. He was an imposing character, about 300 lbs, black beard and bore a striking resemblance to Junior. Pierre, however, was covered in tattoos.

Since the boys were leaving early, they had plenty to do. They spent the next hour or so going over their bikes, making sure fuel and fluid levels were correct. They checked the tire pressure and polished them like new pennies.

The boys then went to the clubhouse and poured over maps. They also spoke to a few members who had made the trip before. After much discussion, it was decided that the best route would be to Niagara Falls, crossing the border, and then taking the I-90 East and then the I-81 South to Springfield. The trip would take about seven hours and they were expected to return the following day.

The motorcycle club they were heading to see was the Harpys. The Harpys were founded in 1967; they were one of the original 1%ers (referring to the fact that 1% of motorcycle gangs were outlaw gangs) and they were based out of Springfield, Pennsylvania.

The boys woke early after little to no sleep. They packed light. They would be leaving their cuts behind. They would be wearing heavy leathers that they had borrowed to protect them from the elements on the road.

The sound of their engines broke the early morning air. It took Tony until after they crossed the Peace Bridge into New York to finally realize that this was actually happening.

The engine was strong, and the wind whistled as it passed his helmet. The feel of the air pushing him down into the seat and the visual that he experienced as he moved down the highway was exhilarating. He could hear Mark's motorcycle on his right and he glanced over to look at Mark's face and realized that he was experiencing the same feelings. They were on their way!

They drove through rolling hills and small towns as Mark and Tony took turns taking the lead. They couldn't believe how fast the miles clicked by. It had been a great run so far. They stopped in a small town on I-81 South to gas up and have some lunch some time before noon. They checked their map to confirm the location of the clubhouse. At this point, they were only an hour or two away from Springfield.

At the gas station they went inside to pay for their gas and buy a sandwich. It was a small station, with not much going on. There was a cute young girl behind the counter, and a guy sitting on a stool a couple of feet behind her who eye-balled Tony and Mark as they came in the door.

The girl thought they were amazing. She'd never seen bikers up close before. She was totally enthralled with Mark's leathers and asked if she could touch them. Mark didn't think anything of it and held out his arm for her. The girl reached for his arm and began stroking the leather.

Tony hadn't noticed, because he was just interested in paying for his gas and sandwiches, but the guy behind the counter was going red in the face and getting really pissed off. This Tony noticed.

He got up off of his stool and started to come around the counter and in a loud voice said "that's my girl you're touching, and I won't stand for it!" He then made the mistake of grabbing for Mark's shoulder and saying "we don't like your kind around here! Get your hand off my girl and get the hell out of the store!" As his hand touched Mark's shoulder, Mark reacted by grabbing him by the arm, bending it behind him and bringing him to his knees and saying "we're members of Lucifer's Army and you don't want to mess with us"! The young man winced in pain and couldn't do anything but stay there. Tony pulled out some money and placed it on the counter. The girl smiled at him, and then Tony turned and with a subtle gesture told Mark they'd had enough fun and they should be on their way.

It turned out that the Harpy's clubhouse was not hard to find. It was located in the industrial outskirts of Springfield. It matched the description that Skip gave them perfectly. It was a large walled compound and had big double gates, which was all you could see from the outside. When they got up closer they saw the Harpy logo on the gate and two cameras pointing towards anything approaching.

Chapter 27

They noted the intercom on the side of the gate and Mark went ahead and pressed the button. There was a moment or two and then a rough voice challenged their reason for being there. "We've been sent by Lucifer's Army, Port Nichols Chapter and we're to ask for Pierre Ladoux. We are Tony Simons and Mark Burns and we are here to pick up a carburetor."

Tony took his finger off the button and waited. A few minutes later the big gates started opening inward and there in the middle of the compound stood the unmistakable Pierre Ladoux, flanked by six Harpys ready for business if things went bad. They could already see the tattoos covering his muscular forearms.

Recognition showed on Pierre's face "I remember the two of you! Prospects!" he said with a hint of disdain. "Doesn't Kevin have any real men to send down here?" The boys didn't know how to react to Pierre's banter. They were, after all, visitors. "We came to pick up the carburetor, but you already know that."

Pierre let out a thunderous laugh, went over to the boys and slapped each one of them on the back. "Where are our manners, take these boys in and give them a beer! Let them wash the road out of their throats."

The tension in the courtyard subsided. The Harpys knew these guys weren't a threat, as they moved in and circled the guys, slapping them on the back and asking them all kinds of questions about their club and the trip. Tony and Mark then followed the welcoming committee into the clubhouse.

The clubhouse was not unlike theirs. There were pool tables, dartboards, a jukebox and a large bar. The bar had a huge Harpy flag hanging behind it. The room was well-lit, and like the Lucifer's Army clubhouse it had the feel of plenty of use. Pierre let them know that they were welcome and that they had a room to crash in for the night. Just then they moved over to the bar and Pierre yelled "Hey Betty we've got some road thirsty visitors!"

From around the corner they could hear a voice say "get the beers yourself! I'm not your maid!" as she then appeared. She didn't recognize them right away. To her they were two more bikers. Tony's stomach did a flip and a smile appeared on his face. They locked eyes as she recognized him. All the memories came flooding back.

Pierre noticed the exchange but didn't say anything. His sister was her own person. She moved closer to the bar and handed out beers. As she got to Tony, she looked him right in the eye and said "what the hell are you doing here?" Tony smiled back and said "just making a parts run. We need to get a carburetor back to Kevin. We leave in the morning." She took all this information in. Pierre said "let's take our beers to the table and talk some business."

Tony was the last to leave and as he turned to walk away Betty said to him with a smile in her eyes "try not to get under foot while you're here."

At the table the bikers talked of Lucifer's Army, Mark and Tony's time with them and the relationship with the Harpys. They asked the boys if they'd been in any good fights and asked about their bikes. When Pierre last saw them he understood they had shit bikes and they saw that they were now driving Harleys. The boys were only too happy to explain how they had built them from scratch. Then one of the Harpys noted that they needed fresh beers.

Since Tony was a Prospect, he volunteered to get them. He sauntered over to the bar where Betty was still standing. Tony asked "did you miss me?" Betty's face hardened and then softened "hadn't given you a second thought! Did you miss me?" Tony smiled back at her "you bet your ass I did! Can we get together later? Maybe go for a ride?" She seemingly thought about it for a second, smiled and said "it's possible." Tony said "let me know when you're done, and we can catch up." He winked, grabbed a bunch of beers and went back to the table.

Later in the evening, after eating and having a few more beers Mark was pulled away from the group by a couple of Harpys that wanted a closer look at his bike. He was only too happy to oblige. This left Tony and Pierre and one other at the table. It seemed to Tony that the two were talking a little more seriously about shop. Tony excused himself from the table and sauntered back to the bar.

He sat at the end of the bar and was finishing his beer when Betty appeared, "ready to call it a night?" "Were you waiting long?" she said. Tony said "forever. Can we get out of here?" She threw her arm over his shoulder and said "you bet." Out the door they went. No one left in the bar paid them any attention.

As they stepped into the night air, Tony turned and took her into his arms and kissed her deeply. She returned the embrace. Tony said "you know I missed you, don't you?" She squeezed him one more time and they both moved towards their motorcycles and mounted their machines. As the engines roared, Betty yelled "follow me!"

The two powerful Harleys sped out of the gates in unison. Tony could see that they were heading toward downtown Springfield. The streets began to lighten up as the street lights came into view.

Betty was slightly ahead of him leading the way and Tony didn't mind because he was busily watching her maneuver the Harley she rode so skillfully. Tony noticed how comfortable she seemed to be on the bike. The bike reacted seamlessly to her every move. Tony had a hard time keeping his eyes on the road.

He noticed that they were heading right into the middle of town. Even at this late night, the traffic seemed to be somewhat heavy. People were walking around, restaurants were still open and people were sitting at tables on the sidewalk.

As they slowed down to stop at a red light he could smell coffee from a nearby café. The light went green and they proceeded through. They continued on through the main streets of Springfield. After a few minutes they came to what looked like the last light before leaving the city and Betty made a left turn. It seemed to be a secondary street that had shops on it such as gas stations and repair shops. The area looked older, but still clean by most standards. Betty slowed, turned down a side street, and stopped at what looked like a small hardware store.

They rolled the bikes around the back and stopped on a parking pad next to a set of stairs. They shut the bikes down and climbed off to stretch themselves. Tony looked at Betty and asked "what do we have here?" Betty said "home sweet home Prospect!"

Tony took the jab and didn't really mind. They climbed the stairs to the second floor, unlocked the door and entered Betty's apartment.

Tony didn't know what to expect. He wondered if it would look like the bike club. When Betty turned the lights on he realized it was far from. It was as neat as a pin, and bigger than he thought it would be. The furniture was well used, but tasteful. It consisted of a large room with a kitchen of sorts at one end and along the other side were two other rooms that Tony guessed were a bedroom and bath. The main living area was in the centre.

The thing that really stood out for Tony, though, were the colourful drawings on the walls and the table that had sketch books spread out. Betty told him to make himself at home as she headed for the kitchen. Tony started wandering around the living area, looking closer at the pictures on the walls and noted that they were really well done and had her signature on them. They were drawings of dragons, mystical warriors, lightning bolts and even unicorns and butterflies.

He also noticed a Harley gas tank sitting on a shelf with the Harpy club logo airbrushed in much detail on it. Tony was impressed and a little taken aback. He did not know that Betty was so artistic. She seemed to constantly surprise him. He moved over to the table with the sketchbooks and saw that there was more of the same.

Betty walked up behind him and handed him a beer. He told her he was amazed at her drawings and asked if she had done the gas tank. She told Tony that she had been drawing for years, but she hadn't thought of it seriously. Then a friend of hers, T.L., saw her work and asked her to come down to her small detailing shop and maybe do some airbrush work for her. Betty said she had started going in a couple of months ago, did a few small pieces for T.L. and she let her practice on the gas tank.

Tony was completely amazed, and told her so. They then moved over to the couch where Betty cozied up to Tony and they kissed. They made attempts at finishing their drinks but before they knew it, dawn was breaking and it was time to go back to the clubhouse.

When they got back it was still quiet. Betty made coffee and they sat at one of the tables to talk about the trip back. Soon after Mark appeared and gave Tony a quizzical stare and then Pierre came in carrying the carburetor. The clubhouse was coming alive and it was time for Tony and Mark to say their goodbyes and leave. There was no need to say goodbye to Betty, they had already said all they needed to.

Taking the carburetor from Pierre, Tony thanked him and turned to Mark and said "let's go."

They walked out into the courtyard, mounted their hogs anticipating the ride back. Mark took the lead first. They headed out by way of the small town they had stopped in when they had the altercation and decided to pass right by.

The trip back was comfortable and now familiar. They did stop once again for gas and food but this time it was uneventful. They felt the need to get back to Port Nichols as fast as they could so as to hand over the carburetor.

The boys happened on a bit of rainy weather on the way, but it didn't last long and it only made them more intent on returning. They didn't speak much during breaks about one another's experiences with the Harpys, but agreed the trip was well worth it and they felt like seasoned bikers.

They passed through the border, again no problems. Then they headed for home. They passed through the gates of the club compound and rolled to a stop in front of Skip. They shut the bikes down, dismounted, retrieved the carburetor and handed it over to him. Mission accomplished. However, Skip didn't feel that way apparently and said "we expected you hours ago Prospects!"

Chapter 28

It was all about the club, everything they had was due to the club. Things seemed really good, but they weren't looking at the whole picture. The club had expanded in what seemed to Tony "overnight." He hadn't realized it.

There was no denying the club had enemies, they were always bumping heads with a club called The Eastern Lords out of Montreal. There were skirmishes. Some club members would be in a bar and out of nowhere all hell would break loose. It would finally end up as a turf war each claiming the bar as their own. Fires were set to trucks, or they'd catch a couple of club members who were away from the rest of the club and beat them to the ground. That would start retributions. It never seemed to end. They were trying to take over the warehouse district on the east side of Toronto. Everybody was trying to expand. Things were escalating out of control.

Tony noticed that on top of the gang importing more weapons for resale, the gang was arming itself. Tensions were running high. He was unsure of what was going to happen next. This was the circle of gang life as the summer moved towards fall.

On top of this, the sponsors of the ex-Lone Wolf Prospects, Peter and Floyd, noticed that they were absent more than once. They were becoming suspicious. They needed to know what they were up to.

The sponsors brought this to Skip's attention and they were ordered to pay closer attention and report back to him. Before this could happen, Skip got a call from the Security Company that was guarding their warehouse. The warehouse had been broken into and a bunch of merchandise was missing or destroyed.

Skip and two of the club members drove out to the warehouse. They talked to the Security people before entering to look around. Once they entered they found that the high-priced merchandise; the guns, pharmaceuticals along with electronic equipment were gone and the rest was destroyed.

The warehouse was again secured, and the three club members returned to the clubhouse and called for a council meeting. Everyone was to attend, there would be no exceptions. Everyone was given two hours notice.

Once Kevin saw that everyone seemed to be there, he called the roll. It wasn't hard to notice that the two ex-Lone Wolves were not there, along with their two sponsors who were supposed to watch them.

There was then some discussion as to who might have seen them last and did anyone give them permission to leave. There were no answers forthcoming.

A few minutes later, Kevin was called to an urgent phone call. Floyd was calling and he told Kevin that the ex-Lone Wolf Prospects were indeed traitors. Their darkest fears had been realized.

The sponsor on the phone told Kevin that they had followed the Prospects to Burlington, to a bar, and waited outside. Ten minutes later, to their surprise, four Eastern Lords and a small transport truck came into the parking lot and stopped. He told Kevin that they watched as the group, including the truck driver went into the bar.

They were very suspicious of these guys and this truck and decided to check things out. They snuck out to the backdoor of the truck; they rolled up the back door to discover it was loaded with guns, pharmaceuticals and electronic equipment.

One of them slipped into the backdoor of the bar, peaked in and saw the Eastern Lords and the two Prospects at the same table, seemingly congratulating each other. The sponsors then made the call at the telephone booth just outside the bar. Kevin was listening intently with anger and disbelief. He then ordered them to disable the bikes and truck and to fall back and wait; the gang was coming!

What the sponsor did not hear was the ex-Lone Wolves telling their new partners that they felt they had been watched and maybe even followed. This alarmed the Eastern Lords and they decided to call for backup to protect their new found merchandise.

Meanwhile after Kevin spoke to the sponsor he slammed the phone down, turned to the members and told them they were going to war! They mobilized quickly and in a moment's notice they were roaring down the highway toward the bar.

The sponsors were just about finished disabling the bikes and truck. It had been about a half an hour. All at once they got jumped from behind! One of the Eastern Lords had come out to check on things and happened on the two sponsors as they were flattening the tires on the truck.

He grabbed one of the sponsors and started beating on him. Before the other sponsor had time to react, the others were coming out of the bar towards them. Just as they were being pounded on by the traitors, the night became lit up by light and sound as Kevin, Skip and 80 angry members of Lucifer's Army roared into the parking lot and stopped in front of the violent altercation. The rest of the Army encircled the men in the parking lot and waited.

Everything went silent. Kevin spoke up "no one touches a member of the Army and if that's our merchandise in that truck, you bastards are not going to make it out of here!"

Just then the sound rang out anew with roaring engines and blinding lights! The Eastern Lords had arrived! Seeing that their members were surrounded by around a hundred of their enemy, they reacted immediately and small pockets of fights broke out all over as more of the bike gang members arrived at the bar. The sound of more than 100 motorcycles, ridden by large angry men had put the area's residents on alert and they would surely call the police.

The Lords rushed the centre of the group trying to get to their members and pull them to safety. This was to no avail. It was seen as an attack by the Army and an all out war ensued. There was mayhem in the parking lot.

The police finally arrived, but with only three cars. Seeing the mass of angry bikers and the war that was getting worse by the minute, they stayed back and called for backup.

It didn't take long for more than a dozen more police cars to show up, but they were not yet organized. They tried to encircle the area in order to contain the bikers. This was a serious mistake.

There was fighting everywhere at one level or another. People were getting hurt or worse. At that time, some of the bikers saw what the police were trying to do, and charged the cruisers, smashing the windows and turning the cars over, as the police ran for cover.

The bikers set two of the cruisers on fire and that was when the authorities started to throw teargas to break up the mob. This didn't work either, it only incited further violence. At this point the police were trying to stay alive.

Gunfire could be heard from the bar area and both clubs rushed inside, weapons ready. There was insanity in the bar. A major fight had broken out and people died on both sides. It was almost impossible to get the Army's dead and injured out of the bar so as not to let the police have them. Eventually they were removed to the club's van.

The Lords were setting fire to the Army's bikes by shooting the gas tanks. This caused them to respond in kind. It was moving from a gang fight to a full out war with no end in sight.

Tony was with Mark and two other guys and everything was going nuts. Out of nowhere, a couple of guys jumped them and the one who was fighting with Tony had some kind of pipe that he was flailing around at him.

Mark got punched to the ground and they broke his arm.

Tony kept looking for some kind of weapon, as he had not yet reached for his gun. Another Lord member took a swing at Tony with a pipe but missed. Tony pounded the man in the gut, and then drove his knee in the side of his head as he was going down. Tony kept beating on him until he got the pipe away from him. Two members of the Army showed up and were now protecting Mark, who was on the ground writhing in pain.

Tony kept swinging the pipe at anyone who was getting close to him. At this point, to Tony, things were moving in slow motion. He felt like he was on the outside looking in. This couldn't really be happening. He was riding on adrenalin and he had been fighting for what seemed like forever. Suddenly, someone hit him from behind and he did a slow motion fall to the ground.

Things went dark. He was out; he wasn't sure for how long. When he came too, two of his club members were dragging him back to his bike. He wasn't all there. He had a nasty bump on the back of his head and a large cut behind his ear. There was still a lot of shit going on around him as he was being dragged out of the battle ground.

The Army members got Tony to his bike. One of them, a rather tall native guy was trying to get his attention, but he was still out of it. Tony finally recognized him; it was Junior. He could hear him keep saying "get on your bike; get on your bike, Tony!"

Tony couldn't grasp what he was saying still. Then Junior hauled off and slapped him across the face, trying to make him come to. Tony thought he was going to lose his teeth, the slap was so hard. That got his attention! He snapped back into the present. Junior told him to get on his bike and Fuck off because this place was going to erupt.

Tony wanted to stay. Junior looked at Tony and again told him to get away! Get away! Tony knew Junior was trying to protect him and finally pulled himself together and drove away, not looking back.

Chapter 29

Tony drove for what seemed like hours. He couldn't decide if he should go back. He couldn't believe he had been in that kind of a nightmare, because that was what it was, a nightmare.

As he drove down the highway he started asking himself why he left. He kept wondering if Mark and Skip were okay. He couldn't believe how a fight like that could start so quickly and he knew that he played a part. He had hurt a lot of people that night and he was agonizing about how he felt about it. He kept asking himself if this would now be his normal.

It was early morning and Tony kept on driving until he realized he needed gas. He happened to be in the Oakville area. He stopped at a small gas station. There wasn't an inch of his body that wasn't cut or bruised. He was a mess. His clothes were torn and he was bloody and filthy. Some of the blood was probably not even his own.

He slid off the bike and noticed his hands were cut and bleeding. He started to pump gas. He was aware that an old station wagon had driven up on the other side of the pump. Someone got out and was proceeding to pump gas as well.

At some point, Tony looked up and noticed that there was a family in the car, a modest-looking woman and two children of about five and six. At just that time, the kids began to notice him and they started screaming in terror. Tony could see the fear in the eyes of the man and his wife and the terror stricken kids. The man stared at him and said "please don't hurt us."

Tony had been through the worse time of his life, but he was devastated at the thought that ordinary people and kids were afraid of him. He asked himself a question: "is this what you have become?" He then walked to the gas station bathroom and looked at himself in the mirror. He didn't recognize the reflection. He knew at that moment he no longer wanted to be that big bad biker.

After washing his face Tony paid for his gas and then he sat on his bike in the parking lot for what seemed to be hours. He just sat there thinking. He thought about all the things that had gone on with the club and it was hard for him to think of it as being all bad. He also felt, at his core, that he wasn't a bad person and yet, here he was, terrorizing families.

Eventually he got back on the road with no plans or destination in mind. He ended up in a sleazy motel on the side of the highway where he thought he'd be safe. He bought a bottle of whiskey and tried to drown out the previous 24 hours. He got numb, but not near drunk, and the nightmares continued. He had a lot to consider.

He eventually ended up back at the club house at about 11:30 the next night. He hadn't slept in two days.

The clubhouse was a war zone. It felt very dangerous. There was a lot of drinking, drugs, anger and screaming. A lot of the guys wanted to go out again, find the Lords and finish it.

Tony wasn't sure where Skip and Kevin were yet. Tony was too tired to get involved so he went into the back to get some sleep. He could hear the fighting and arguing but he soon faded out. He woke the next day, unsure of the time, but the clubhouse had finally quieted somewhat.

He found out that in the middle of the night, half the members drove out to try and find the Lords. There were still about 20 guys left talking. Tony didn't say anything, but got in closer so he could hear what was being said. He found out that two of their brothers were killed that night. Junior was one of them. He couldn't believe his ears. Junior was the one who saved him. He was the one who told him to get away.

Tony found out that the standoff had lasted until dawn when the police finally gained control of the situation. Skip was taken to the hospital under police escort and the Lords' Chapter Leader was put in a cruiser and that was the last anyone saw of him. There were also a lot of members in jail from both Lucifer's Army and the Lords. Lots of other guys were in the hospital, including Mark.

Tony felt sick to his stomach; he got up, got on his bike and drove down the highway ending up in Niagara Falls. He spent two days there, in a motel room. He needed time to think about everything that had happened. Could he continue on this path? Could he get involved in something like this or worse again? Yes, the trip he and Mark took had been thrilling, there was no denying that. He felt free and the road was amazing. This was part of motorcycle club life, but it wasn't all. There was the family aspect, but there was a price to be paid for being a part of this family.

He also knew that he was getting close to fulfilling what would lead him to become a full patch member. He now was not sure whether he was willing or capable of paying that price. No, he couldn't see it.

He thought about all the other guys in the club. Some were getting on, had been there for years and years and it was all they knew. There was nowhere for them but the club. Tony thought they looked dead, there was nothing else but where they were. They knew nothing else.

Tony didn't want to look like that, couldn't see himself doing this for the next 20 – 30 years. He wasn't sure that if he stayed he'd even live that long.

Chapter 30

After a couple of days Tony drove back to the club, but it was different this time. He was different. For once he was clear headed. Right now, the club was the only place he could go, but he would come up with a plan. There were no bright lights or bells telling him how, but he knew he wasn't going to terrorize a kid again.

Things had calmed down at the clubhouse by then, there were police outside the compound keeping an eye on things, checking the bikers as they went in and out. He stayed mainly to himself, just listening. He was trying to find out what, if anything, they were planning. Mark had gotten out of the hospital and had been shuttled to the clubhouse in the van.

Tony wasn't sure what to say to him when he returned. He was sitting at a table having a beer when Mark came in, still looking quite a mess. He came over to Tony's table with a beer. He was hot, breathing fire; he was so mad. He was planning on paying them back and nothing was going to stop him, not even a broken arm.

Tony and Mark had discussed leaving the club, in general terms long before the fight. But now Mark was hot and it seemed, at least right now, that was not his plan. He was speaking loudly and wildly. He said that he, Skip and Tony were going to take down the Eastern Lords. "Just kill them all." Just like Tony, the fight had changed him, but in the opposite way. He was ranting and raving on how he was going to create all this damage. He was looking at Tony, expecting approval, and for Tony to chime in with agreement.

Mark finally got pissed off when Tony didn't join in and confronted him. "Tony, what the hell is going on with you?" Tony confessed to Mark about how scared he had been during the fight. That he had fought to survive and had hurt a lot of people. He wasn't proud of what he had done. Tony told Mark how Junior had pulled him out of the fight after he had been knocked out and didn't remember too much after that. He did know that guys had died, and Junior was one of them.

Mark calmed down after that. He hadn't realized that they had lost members. They looked at each other in silence for some time.

Chapter 31

The club was still in shock after the war with the Lords and the loss of two of its members. A lot of the guys were still recovering from their wounds or just getting out of the local lockup after making bail. Mark had a cast on his arm and would not be riding for the better part of two months, but he was still mad as hell at having been beaten that way without getting his licks in. This he vowed would come later.

Rick and Skip made bail, but would be back in court at a later time to answer for the club's crimes. The members that were healthy enough to be at the club were there discussing the activity of late and what was to come.

It was hard to get your head around the fact that you had lost two close friends and brothers to slime like the Lords. This act of war would be paid for ten times over when the time was right. That was for later. The brothers were to be celebrated and homage was to be paid for those who had fallen.

The bodies of the fallen were handed over to a funeral home with little or no questions, seeing that one of the members worked there and a stack of cash goes a long way to getting things done.

Junior and Tim Sykes' bodies were cremated quickly and the club was given the ashes to do with what they saw fit. It was decided that the ashes would be released into the winds going down the QEW Highway at 100 mph with as many club members as they could get on bikes. The boys would have loved the send off.

Word went out to all the clubs that were affiliated with the Army or had done business with the club that a wake was being put together for a couple of fallen members. Fellow bikers could participate if they knew the boys and wanted to drink a beer or two in their memory.

Word came back quickly from coast to coast that many brothers and sisters that knew Junior and Tim would indeed be there for that ride. Condolences also came from the States and many riders would be there for the boys' last run.

Tony and two other Prospects were given the task of gathering up as much beer and liquor as was possible in anticipation of what was to happen in three days' time. Tony stayed as busy as possible and tried not to think about what had happened to him and what questions were raging in his head. Right now it was about Junior and Tim.

The club reserved the entire top floor of a local hotel to make sure that the out-of-towners could stay close. Kevin had received a call from the Club President in Toronto saying that they'd be sending a couple of representatives to show support. This was going to be a big sendoff!

Tony and Mark looked at each other in amazement, thinking about what was going to happen in just a couple of days. Saturday would be the sendoff.

The rooms in the clubhouse filled quickly as did any openings at the Franklin. Mo was told to expect a wave of new customers and he stated that he would "stand first round" to the whole group in memory of Junior and Tim. He also stated that he would turn the bar over to the club for the night of the wake.

Plans were set into motion and Saturday came very quickly. The club was now some 200 strong and comprised of 10 different clubs from Vancouver to Newfoundland, New York State to Pennsylvania.

Tony and Mark knew some of the guests, but not near half. Most were full patch riders and had little time for Prospects that seemed to get in the way.

The club compound and parking lots were full to capacity and then some. There was a lot of greeting going on, but they were there for the funeral ride and the wake later.

The local police were in full force, but stayed back in order to let the procession move out and the ceremony begin. They did not want a recurrence of a short time ago.

Kevin and Skip started their bikes and that set the deepening rumble into motion. The air was alive with 200 waking monsters and the smell of exhaust filled the air. With all this going on and the amount of people that began to move, Tony finally caught site of Betty. She was near the front of the procession, near Kevin and Skip. She did look back for a second and caught Tony's eye. A tip of her helmet and she was gone.

The gangs headed out to the highway and formed up two by two. The group took over the QEW Southbound and accelerated to an evil speed and deafening roar. The Harleys roared down the blacktop; 80, 90, 100 mph!

Needless to say traffic on the QEW yielded the right of way to the advancing extraordinary procession of motorcycles.

Then it was time. Skip had strapped Junior's ashes to the side of his bike on an angle, Rick had Tim's ashes lined up in the same manner. In a second the tops were opened and the screaming winds tore the ashes from the urns into the sky. In a matter of seconds it was over. The large group sounded their horns in a final goodbye. Tony was near the back of the pack and he too sounded his horn and felt his stomach tighten as he said goodbye to the man that had saved his life.

Kevin then turned the procession around and headed back to the clubhouse. The building filled quickly and the compound overflowed with gleaming metal and club leathers.

The bar was relocated outside and swelled to over capacity in minutes. It was hard for Tony to hear what was going on because everyone was talking at once. Tony spotted Betty receiving condolences from many club members and moved to her side to add his. Betty looked at him and took his hand. Her question was simple. "You were with him?" Tony said "yes" and told her that Junior had saved his life by putting him on his bike and telling him to go. She nodded her head and started to move away. "We have to talk later." Tony silently nodded and moved to the bar to begin his duties.

It was a celebration like none other and much was said about Junior and Tim and their antics with the club all these years. Guys remembered the good and the bad times that they had had with them. All decided that they wouldn't have had it any other way. They said that they would be greatly missed. Their cuts were to be hung over the bar in the clubhouse and Tony imagined that many a toast would be given to Junior and Tim for many years to come. Then Kevin got cup and made a toast to the fallen members and vowed they would not be forgotten.

Before the celebration really got rolling, all that were there unanimously agreed that Junior's bike would be auctioned off and the monies gathered would be sent to Betty. She had a bike already but could use the cash. Then the party really ramped up.

Tony watched Betty all night as she moved around the massive bikers and could hardly wait to get her alone to talk to her. This came sooner than he had thought as Betty walked right up to him and said "can we get out of here?"

They stepped into the night and mounted their Harleys. Gunning the engines together this time, Tony said over the noise "this time you follow me." They roared into the night with Tony slightly in the lead. He really liked being with her. They sped through town down the main street and made their way down to the harbour. They drove along the sea wall out to the lighthouse and back around to Tony's rooming house. There he stopped, stepped off the hog and waited for Betty to shut down.

"This isn't the Hilton I've taken you to, but I call it home right now." Tony opened the door to a staircase leading to a narrow hallway and stepped in. As they moved down the hall, Mo stuck his head out of his room door and noticed Betty right away. He smiled, nodded to Tony and closed his door. Tony looked at Betty and said "a friend," as he opened his own door, down the hall.

They fell into each other's arms and nothing more was said until hours later when they were sitting on the edge of the bed looking at each other.

"I have to tell you something Tony" she said. "I have left the bike club. The only future I saw coming for myself there was as someone's biker bitch and spending the rest of my life wondering if I could have done better." Tony was shocked, but listened intently.

"T.L. and I have teamed up and have become partners in her detailing shop. She really likes my artwork and sees it catching on in a big way. People have already placed orders for having their rides air-brushed. I know that this is what I was meant to do." Tony smiled and nodded his head.

"Since we are telling secrets, I have one myself. I am going to be leaving Lucifer's Army before I am asked to patch up and commit to something I know in my gut I cannot do. I know I owe them, but I have to leave."

They looked at each other, knowing that this was the last time they would be together and it was for the best. They rested for an hour and then without saying a word, they rose, got dressed and left the room.

Back at the clubhouse many had left to return to where they had come from and Betty was saying goodbye to Skip and Kevin. They told her to be safe and that they'd be in touch with her.

Betty mounted her hog, quickly glanced at Tony and drove away with Pierre and a few other club members that had rode in with her. Tony watched as she faded into the distance.

When the wake was finally over, the clubhouse looked like a tornado had hit it. It was the responsibility of all the Prospects to do the clean up. When Tony finally arrived back at the rooming house he was exhausted.

As he walked in he was thinking about the last time he had been there and that Betty had been there with him. He walked past the table by the window and noticed a large envelope. He opened it and found a drawing that he had seen before, in Betty's apartment. There was also a note that stated. "This is one of the drawings you were admiring when you were in Springfield. I hope you will think of me when you look at it."

Chapter 32

For the next couple of weeks it was fairly quiet. The police finally left and some of the guys were busy with court dates. Tony guessed this was the stuff that happened after a gang war. He knew he was on his way out, he just didn't know how, where, or when. He asked himself constantly "what do you do after all this? What can you do after all this?" He was supposed to be a big bad biker living in a biker club, but he knew inside he was a fraud. At the same time he was Tony Simons living outside Toronto looking for a way to get out of yet another situation. So in some ways, he was back to the start. It was quite an eye-opener.

He was in this state of mind for what seemed like forever. He was in a cloud. He didn't know what to do. He didn't know anything but the club or back at home. He knew without a doubt he wasn't going to be that "Simons kid" again. For one thing, he was a man now, his own man.

Tony knew he'd have to wait for the right time to leave. The club was gearing up for another run at the Lords. They were making plans and this time incorporating other bike clubs. It was going to be another all out war.

A call came from the Club President in Toronto wanting Kevin and Rick to come to the Club Headquarters to discuss the future of their chapter of Lucifer's Army as a whole and the up and coming war with the Lords. Kevin and Rick were to leave immediately and prepare for detailed discussions on what was to come.

Tony wasn't sure when the war against the Lords was going to take place, that was a secret. He thought that it probably wouldn't be much longer after the Toronto meeting. It scared him and he knew he didn't want any part of it. Time was of the essence.

Chapter 33

A couple of the members were still in the hospital and Tony and a few other brothers were going to go and check in on them. They were bringing them a bottle of booze. Since the hospital was right downtown, they were riding down Main Street which was the most direct route. In doing so they had to pass the armory. This was a place that young cadets learned the finer points of being in the military. They learned to take direction and work as a team.

As the riders rolled by, Tony found himself watching a group of cadets going through a drill. For some reason this activity held his interest and he pulled over to watch. Tony noticed that the cadets were being directed by a Drill Sergeant. He was in the process of giving them commands and the cadets were doing their best to obey. Tony watched them work as a team as they listened intently to the Sergeant.

Tony continued to watch for about five minutes and then realized he should catch up to the other guys. He continued to think about what he saw. As he turned a corner heading toward the hospital he glanced up to see a sign "There's No Life Like It." It had a picture of a young soldier in full uniform, saluting the flag.

The image burned into his mind and he couldn't help thinking about it at the hospital and during the ride back to the club.

The next day Mark and Tony visited Mark's mom in the projects. She had divorced his dad since they had moved her to her tiny townhouse. They loved visiting Mark's mother. It was a place they could take a breath from club life and maybe get a home cooked meal. Olive always enjoyed seeing the boys. The boys could also keep an eye on her in case the old man gave her any trouble.

They found themselves sitting on the steps on this warm sunny day, having a beer. They were talking about all kinds of stuff, really nothing at all. They were jabbing at each other. Tony said Mark looked like a piece of shit with his broken arm and stitches. Mark said Tony didn't look any better.

They had been sitting there for about half an hour. Tony looked at Mark and realized that they were back in the

projects! It was like nothing had changed. Tony looked at
Mark and asked him what he wanted to be when he grew up.
Mark said he didn't know. Mark asked Tony the same
question. Somehow Mark sensed that this day would come.
Tony needed to move on and maybe become something
great.

Then Mark said "you're leaving the club, aren't you?"
Tony looked him square in the eye and said "yes I am."
Mark wanted to know when this would happen. Tony didn't
know, but he was sure he wasn't going to be a part of the
next campaign.

Mark then admitted to Tony that he couldn't see himself
doing anything but this. His brother was there for him and
had led him into the life. It was all he wanted. He got
satisfaction from the club's dynamics.

Tony looked at Mark and said "I'm scared for you
brother, this upcoming war will be an evil thing. We've been
together for a long time; I have to believe you'll be safe."

They spoke about the town, and how there wasn't any
work, except in the car factory or on the boats. They said
they could probably work in the warehouses for the Italians,
but that wasn't a good idea. Mark said if he wasn't in the
gang, he'd probably be working with his dad in the factory.

Tony sat there thinking about what the other men in the Simons' family did that didn't make them assholes. He went down the list until he got to the previous generation, Tony's grandfather, Ben.

Tony began to smile. His grandfather had been in the military, the Air Force, for 25 years. He of course, retired a long time ago and passed away, but Tony remembered him fondly. He had been in battle, those were the dark times. It had cost him a son who had also been in the military. Tony remembered his Uncle Danny. He had come back from Korea a broken man. He was insane and died in an asylum. The war had changed him. Tony remembered the stories his grandfather told. Though he'd been through rough times, he remembered he always looked happy when he talked about his time in the military.

A feeling washed over him like none he had ever felt before. In that moment he felt as if his grandfather was there and would have been proud. As Tony sat there it seemed to make sense. He looked over at Mark and told him what he was going to do. There needed to be much research done so he had to start now.

Tony was aware that if it didn't work out, he'd have nothing, but he didn't have anything now. So he had to try.

Mark of course, said he thought he was crazy. To which Tony replied that he thought it might be crazy too, but he was going to give it a shot. The more he thought about it, the more it made sense.

Tony was aware that he was looking at a fork in the road. He could stay in the club, or try the military. The first choice wasn't really a choice at all. He'd wind up in jail, dead or living in a trailer with his friend Mark. He'd have to do a lot of drugs to get him through what he would need to do to stay. This was not the life he wanted.

He needed more information before he could make any moves, but they sat there for what seemed like hours, talking about what it might be like. At some point they left the steps.

Chapter 34

The Recruitment office was in Hamilton. Early the next morning Tony left his cut in his room and drove his motorcycle into Hamilton to the Recruiting Station.

The recruitment office was in a large building but the office itself was open and visible to the street. Tony walked in feeling nervous with anticipation. It was an open-door situation; there was a counter where a man in uniform asked if he needed help. There were cubicles behind the counter. Tony told him that he wanted information on joining the military. The man in uniform directed him to a cubicle. There he met a Master Corporal Johns who stood up, smiled and offered his hand to greet Tony. He asked him to sit down and asked what they could do for him.

Tony told him that he needed more information about the military before he could make any decisions. The Master Corporal asked him "why the military?" Tony told him that he thought this was where he needed to be in his life. He told him that his grandfather and uncle both had served and he was proud of them.

They talked for a couple of hours about the service, Tony's grandfather, and being part of a team. Tony noticed the Master Corporal's confidence and heard his passion. He needed this. The Master Corporal took him into another small room and turned on a movie for him to watch. It was about military service, being part of a bigger team, and that there was "no life like it". At the end of the movie, Tony came back to the cubicle and asked the Master Corporal what he needed to do next, he was interested.

The Master Corporal told Tony to think about what he had learned, and if he really was interested, he was to fill in the application, and give him a call. Tony walked out with a pile of pamphlets and a package containing application forms.

Tony drove back to Port Nichols and stopped by a bar to have a beer and think about what had just happened. He wasn't going to go to the club for the rest of the day. He had too much on his mind.

Two days later and after much soul-searching Tony began filling in the forms. What could it hurt to just submit the application? Maybe they would just reject it and it would all have been for not.

When he drove back to Hamilton the following day Tony asked for the same recruiter to talk to. When he went into the cubicle, the Master Corporal gave Tony a quick smile. "I wasn't sure if we'd be seeing you again, Tony." Tony was surprised that the Master Corporal remembered his name. "I just thought I'd drop this off to see if it meets the force's requirements."

The Master Corporal took the bulky package of forms and said that he would be submitting them that day. It would still take a week to get the results back. If they were going to proceed further, Tony would get a call to come in for testing. If he did not meet the requirements, he would get a letter. Tony stood up and started to leave. The Master Corporal stood up also, shook his hand and said "good luck."

Tony had given the recruiter Olive's phone number and address so he could be contacted. It was going to be a long week.

Tony went back to the club the next day and drilled down into his duties like he'd never been away. Mark was glad to see that he was there. He noticed that Tony pretty much kept to himself.

The club was abuzz because of the meeting in Toronto and what was coming.

On the morning of the third day around 11 o'clock, Tony was polishing a member's bike and deep in thought. He didn't hear Mark coming up behind him. Mark whispered in his ear, "hey you little shit; mom got a call this morning from some guy at a recruiting office. He wants you to phone him today. You are really going to do this, aren't you?" Tony only smiled.

As soon as Tony could steal away, he ran over to the Franklin and asked Mo if he could use the phone. He called the recruiting office and was told that his application had been approved and that if he wished to proceed, he was to show up at the recruiting office in two days at 7:00 AM, for further testing and evaluations. They also told Tony that failing any of the tests would mean rejecting his application.

Tony's head was in the clouds. Was it possible? He went back to the club to try and work. Mark was all over him with questions. Tony only said that they were moving forward with his application, but he still had a way to go.

The next day, Kevin returned from Toronto and called a club meeting for that night. The place was packed and questions were flying everywhere. The meeting was called to order and the place fell silent. Kevin told the members that the President of the seven chapters was really pissed that the Lords had invaded their turf and killed two members in a war at the bar. He was also angry at the fact that two spies had managed to infiltrate the club and caused all the shit that happened.

The President was calling out all the Chapters for a full out war with the Lords, and it was going to happen quickly. Kevin told the club to stand ready to move on the Lords at the President's orders.

Tony was listening intently to what Kevin was saying and watched the reactions of the members, knowing that this war was coming. He found that he was not reacting like the rest of the group of angry bikers and sat at a table sipping a beer. This did not go unnoticed by Skip or Mark and they looked at each other with questioning eyes. Skip remembered noticing Tony's actions over the last week or two were different than everyone else's. Skip noted to himself that he was going to pay more attention to his Prospect. In that respect, he asked one of the members to follow him around and report back.

The day of testing and evaluations found Tony up before dawn. He was unable to sleep most of the previous night. He left his cut in his room and assumed the part of a recreational rider, heading to Hamilton. He wasn't paying much attention during the ride or he would have seen a motorbike some distance behind him.

He got to the government building early but hung close by until it opened. He was not alone. Around 30 young men, about Tony's age were there also. The unknown rider that Tony failed to notice earlier had parked a few blocks away and turned off his engine.

The doors opened and the men moved in and were guided to a large room. There were at least eight military men in the room, one who looked to be in charge.

"Listen up!" the one man said. "My name is Captain Porter. When I call your name, you'll be directed to the left or right side of this room. From there, your squad will be under the direction of the men assigned to you and your testing will begin."

Tony only had time for a quick look at the guys in his "squad." Tony said to himself "what's a squad?" That's what they were calling the group he was in. They were all "normal" looking guys, of all shapes and sizes. Some were so skinny you could just about see through them. There were large men with long hair and a few short ones with beards. Some looked like they worked out a lot, but most did not. Tony thought he looked pretty average.

They were tested all morning on the physical part of the evaluation. They did sit-ups, pushups, running on a treadmill; some guys puked, but Tony made a passing mark.

Two were asked to leave immediately. Then there were strength tests, lift tests, everything you could imagine. Medicals were performed on the group; from nose to toes, looking for abnormalities. Two guys were asked to leave after this as well, because of irregular heart rates or blood pressure problems. There were eye tests, breathing tests, and tests Tony never heard of before. It had been a long morning.

It was finally lunch time. As with any military exercise, lunch was provided. Tony had never eaten so well. He lined up with his "squad" and was served from what they called a "field hay box." This was a hot meal, given to soldiers working in the field or during exercises. There were pork chops and gravy, hot potatoes and vegetables, coffee and some kind of cake.

Tony did notice that the other "squad" was kept apart from them until they switched testing areas. The physical part of testing for Tony's "squad" was now done and he was still there. Now the mental testing was to begin including skill and aptitude. Tony couldn't understand why putting round things in square holes under time, was tested; but he did understand that this was to see what he was best suited for.

Tony had originally wanted to be in the navy, but the recruiter said that this would be determined. Skill tests, knowledge tests, and visual reaction tests were completed. Finally there was a psychological evaluation with the resident shrink.

He asked Tony all kinds of personal questions. How did he feel about himself? How did he feel about his family? Did he have friends? Did he like talking to people? What did he like to talk about? The shrink was using big words that Tony sometimes didn't understand. He was getting a little heated by some of them, but tried to answer them truthfully.

Tony was sure, at one point during the interview that the shrink was trying to ask if he was gay, but he wasn't sure and didn't know how to answer. Tony told him in no uncertain terms that he just wanted to belong and do well.

It was an exhaustingly long day. But he was still there. When the day was over, and the group got back together, there was a marked difference in the number of guys that were left. Many were gone.

Captain Porter came to the front of the room and told the group that the testing was complete. He offered his congratulations to the men that were still there. All the testing would be evaluated over the next week and those candidates that were successful would be contacted by phone and given further instruction. Those that failed to measure up to the requirements for the positions opened would receive a letter.

Tony was physically and mentally exhausted. It had been a very long day and now he had to get back to the clubhouse, there was still work to be done, and he was concerned that some of the members might be becoming suspicious about why he was away so much.

He moved out onto the road and down the street to the highway entrance and moved into traffic. If he would not have been so tired, he would have noticed that lone biker trailing behind him.

Getting back to the club took about half an hour. Tony pulled in and went directly to the bar. Mark was already there and pissed. "Where the hell have you been all this time?" Tony didn't answer him and a couple of hours went by with nothing happening.

Tony saw Skip talking to one of the other members and then to Kevin. A minute or so later, Skip came right up to Tony at the bar and told him to meet him at the Franklin in an hour and then he walked away.

Mark looked at Tony and came closer to him. Mark told Tony that Skip had come to him earlier in the day and asked him what was wrong with Tony. Mark told Tony that he had his back and told Skip that he did not know and that Tony was his own man. Tony could feel the walls closing in on him and his fate was sealed.

He left the bar an hour later and headed for the Franklin to meet Skip. There weren't many people there for a Monday night. Tony could see Skip clearly sitting at one of the back tables. That was one long walk across the bar room floor. Tony sat across from Skip and ordered a beer from the waitress.

Skip did not wait to say what needed to be said. "What the hell are you doing? Members are talking about you. This club needs its members to be fully committed at all times, especially now. I vouched for you. I stood up to the members and said that you would be loyal and trustworthy. I did this for you! No one else! You have embarrassed me by not holding to your side of our bargain. I want your cut and your keys! You're done! Get the hell out of here!"

Tony felt the roof come down on his head. It was over. He took his cut off and dropped it on the table along with his keys. It had been one hell of day. Tony was devastated but in some way, relieved. All he knew was that he was tired and needed to go home.

Mo had been watching what was going on and couldn't help but hear. As Tony walked by the bar Mo called him over and in a low voice told him to stay in the room at the back of the bar and he would give him a ride at the end of the shift.

Mo got Tony back to the rooming house at about 2:00 AM During the drive home Mo told Tony that he had heard he was trying to get into the military. He was proud that Tony was trying to better himself. He went on to say that he had an uncle that joined the Army and served his country with pride until he was killed overseas. It wasn't anything Mo could do, but he was proud of Tony because he wanted to join.

When they got to the rooming house Tony opened the door to his room and fell onto his bed. It wasn't until 2:00 PM that afternoon before he opened his eyes. He laid there for the longest time, trying to make sense of yesterday's events. He was numb and caught in the middle of a turning point that he had created. He was no longer that big bad biker wannabe and the unknown possibilities of the military were up in the air. To top it all off, he was afoot. His beautiful ride was gone.

He tried to imagine what would have been if he had just shut up and been satisfied with his life with Lucifer's Army. He breathed deep, there was no future there. It was Tuesday and he wasn't to hear from the recruiter until Friday, if at all. It was going to be a long week.

After Mo drove Tony home he told Liz about what happened with him at the bar. In the afternoon, Liz busied herself with cleaning duties on the tenant floor by dusting and cleaning bathrooms. When she heard Tony moving around, she approached the door and gently knocked. Tony had just been thinking of how he was starving and had not eaten since yesterday at the recruiting centre. He knew he had to remedy that situation quickly, but wasn't sure how. Just then he heard the soft knock at his door.

He opened the door and Liz could see the troubled look on his face. She told him that there was fresh coffee on and something to eat if he was interested. Tony thanked her and said that he would be down as soon as he cleaned up.

As Tony got about half way down the stairs he could smell the fresh brewed coffee and it sent his taste buds on a tail spin. Then there was something else, and it smelled like heaven. He entered the small bright kitchen and Liz was just setting down a bowl of hot steaming home-made soup. Alongside the soup was a large cup of coffee and a sandwich made of thick slices of home-made bread with ham and cheese. His stomach did a happy dance.

Liz smiled at him and asked him to sit down. He did so willingly. Liz had thought Tony had been getting a little tougher in the previous months, but she didn't feel he was quite like the others. Who knows what he would be like if he stayed with the club, but she was pleased that he was at least trying this new route.

Tony hadn't eaten many meals at the rooming house since he started staying there, but she thought she would probably see him at her table a few more times in the coming days. She let him know that supper was at 6:30 PM if he'd like to come. She made small talk, hoping to take his mind off of things even for a few minutes. She mentioned that the November air was becoming chilly in the morning. She also mentioned that she was pleased that Mo had gotten to know him, as he wasn't much for doing that sort of thing.

When Tony was finished, he thanked Liz profusely and headed to his room. He looked over the pamphlets again and found himself a little anxious and nervous. What would he do if he wasn't successful? He did feel that he had a good chance since he got through the testing day when so many others had not. He'd find out soon enough.

He thought it was funny the flip flops his life had taken. His life at home was so incredibly bad, and then he found Mark and the club and felt like he belonged. Then things went sour there with all the fights and ugliness, then the recruitment centre testing where he got through the whole day; then staring Skip in the eye while he told him he wasn't measuring up and ousting him.

Tony was again exhausted from the stress that his mind was going through. He turned the little TV on, lay on the bed and fell asleep. He didn't wake until the next morning. He rose fairly early and headed downstairs and sat at the dining table; the other two tenants were just leaving. Tony had a cup of coffee and headed out.

He walked down to the pier and watched people as they came and went. It was funny to Tony not to have a place to go or work to do. He let his mind wander thinking about what the other people that were around were up to. He tried not to think about the call he was waiting for. His grandmother had always said "a watched pot never boils." He smiled to himself. He hadn't thought of her in quite some time.

He grabbed a hot dog with his meager funds at around noon and continued just wandering. He wound up back at the boarding house just in time for supper. Stew this time, it was amazing. He didn't remember ever eating so well. He wondered why he hadn't had all his meals here.

When he was done he went into his room and turned the little TV on. The next day would be day 3. He knew what he would do. He would go to Olive's and explain to her what he had done and what he was hoping to do. He was sure by now Mark had told her that he was kicked out of the club. But he wanted to explain to her in person, what he was thinking. It was important to him that she did not think badly of him for wanting to leave his friends.

Chapter 35

Tony had never ridden on a bus before, but he had no other choice. He soon came to the realization that only strange people rode the bus. So he sat in the back and tried not to look.

Old people, students and mothers with screaming kids and wannabe bad-ass teenagers used this mode of transportation. Two of the little bad-asses tried to give an elderly lady a bad time. It was a mistake on their part. Tony grabbed one of them as they tried to take her purse. He got up, and threw the little shit into an empty seat, took the purse from him and dared him to make a sound before he got off. The kid cowered in the corner. Tony knew there'd be no more trouble.

The elderly woman thanked him and the bus driver told him that his next ride would be free.

The bus ride took about a half an hour so Tony had time to look out the window and remember that he too had come from this part of town. The run down apartments, small houses and cracked sidewalks, along with their chain linked fences were familiar to Tony. The only difference now was the many empty lots that weren't there before.

His stop was coming up and he recognized the townhouses that he and Mark had ridden by many times before. He got off and walked the half a block to Olive's place. He knew she was home because he could hear the radio in the front room. He didn't knock; Olive had an open-door policy. He found her in the kitchen making a pot of Earl Grey Tea. Olive liked to sip her tea on the front porch and talk to the neighbours as they walked by.

She looked up from her task, recognized Tony and went over and gave him a big hug. "Where the heck have you been Tony? I've been worried sick about you!" Tony said that he would explain later, but he'd been on the bus for quite a while and needed to use the bathroom as he stepped away.

Olive used this time to phone Mark's girlfriend so she could get word to Mark that Tony was there. Olive gave Tony a cup of tea on his return and they both went to the front step to talk.

"I wanted to tell you myself, but I guess you already know. I couldn't do it anymore, Ma. At first it was great, I belonged somewhere, to something, we both did. The deeper I went, the uglier I saw it was. I don't want to steal anymore and I sure as hell don't want to hurt people anymore. I couldn't see myself there long term and so I looked for a way out. I knew there had to be more."

She squeezed his hand and said she was proud of him. It was going to be okay she said.

They sat there for about ten minutes or so and it was getting close to lunch. Olive asked Tony to stay and she got up to go to the kitchen. As she moved into the house, the phone rang. Tony could hear Olive talking on the phone "really? Yes he's here, I'll get him. Tony, it's for you" she said. He took the phone from Olive, looking at her with a questioning stare.

The voice on the other end of the phone was positive and authoritative, "is this Tony Simons? This is Captain Porter at the recruiting centre in Hamilton. I know that we said that the processing could take a week, but we have to get moving on this now. Congratulations Tony! You passed! Currently we have an opportunity for you if you're still interested."

Tony had to remind himself to breath as he listened to what he was hearing. "Interested? You bet I am Captain." Captain Porter then said "we have to move on this now, so you have to be here at the recruitment centre tomorrow morning to complete the process." Tony heard himself saying, yes, he would be there, and thanked the Captain for getting back to him so fast.

He hung up the phone and looked at Olive in amazement. "Holy Christ Ma, I made it!"

Before she could reply, they heard a car stopping in front of the house. Mark jumped out of the car and sprinted up the stairs. As he moved into the house, he knew that he didn't have to ask, just by looking at Tony's face. "Jesus Christ, you made it!"

Tony smiled and started banging Mark on the shoulders "I made it man, I made it!" They spent the next hour or so talking about the tests that Tony passed, and what would be coming in the near future. Tony told Mark that he would find out tomorrow what the offer was, and would talk to him again after he got back from Hamilton.

Mark was still shaking his head in disbelief as he walked out the door to head back to the club. He had told Skip he was going to see their mom and he would need the van, but he hadn't said that Tony would be there. Tony asked Mark to drive him to the rooming house, seeing as it was on the way. Another sleepless night was in front of him, but he didn't care.

Chapter 36

Dawn found Tony on the highway with his thumb out, pointed toward Hamilton. This was something that was new to him also. He had never hitchhiked before. It didn't take long for a family to pick him up and drive him right to the recruiting building after they heard where he was going. This was one family that wasn't terrorized when they offered him a lift.

He had ten minutes to wait until the building opened. He stood there watching military people going inside the building and knew in his stomach that life was about to change.

When the doors finally opened, in he went. There were four others along with Tony that were led to Captain Porter's office at the end of the hall. All five were asked to be seated just outside his office. They were told they would be called in one at a time.

You could see the nervousness on the faces of the men, but that was not a game changer. They were here to enlist.

The door opened and the Captain was standing there in all his finery. He was wearing what Tony found out later was full dress greens, gold braid and metals.

He looked at the group and called "Tony Simons." Tony felt like he was struck by lightning. The Captain led him into his office that contained a desk, flag and a few military pictures. He motioned for Tony to sit down in front of the desk. He moved to sit on the other side. Tony was overwhelmed but stayed still.

There was a moment of silence; then the Captain smiled and reached over to shake his hand. "Congratulations Mr. Simons, as I said before, we'd like to make you an offer." Tony almost fainted. The Captain explained that the opening was in the Air Force Element as an Air Defence Technician, working on radar sites that were sometimes in isolated areas. His aptitude had placed him high on the list and this position was within the scope of that aptitude. Tony was reeling with excitement. Inside he was telling himself "I got an offer!"

The Captain then gave him a copy of the job description and asked him to take a minute and read about what they were asking him to do. All the time this was going on, the

Captain kept asking him if he had any questions. They seemed to care what Tony thought and he liked it.

Tony read the description from cover to cover, committing to memory what was written. Tony then looked up at the Captain, smiled and said "let's do this!" The Captain stood and put his hat on. They then went into a small room off to the side. It had two flags and a large crest on the wall. Tony found out later that this was the Queen's Crest.

The Captain had Tony put his left hand on the Bible and raise his right hand. Tony repeated the Oath of Allegiance as the Captain read the words and at the end Tony said "I do." The Captain shook Tony's hand one more time. He went back to the Captain's office where Tony signed his offer of employment and his oath to the Canadian Military. He was asked to report to the Sergeant of Administration just outside his office.

The Sergeant gave Tony his travel orders and told Tony to follow them to the letter. They consisted of a leave pass, a travel schedule and a list of do's and don'ts during travel. He also gave Tony something called an aide de memoire telling him what to expect at the recruit school, and $200 travel allowance. He was to leave in seven days.

Tony asked the Sergeant if he could get a copy of his Oath of Allegiance. This was not a problem. He thanked the Sergeant for all he had done for him and then left the building. Seven days was not a long time and Tony knew he had many things to do.

He walked down the street to the Bus Station where he purchased a ticket to Port Nichols. Once he arrived, he hopped a local bus and was back at the rooming house sitting in his room, staring out the window in disbelief.

After awhile Tony went down to the kitchen, Liz was at the stove, making lunch for her tenants. She told him to pour himself a cup of coffee and asked him how his day was. The words came rattling out of his mouth faster than he could get them out. He did manage to tell her about what had happened and the fact that he would be leaving in seven days.

Liz was happy and sad at the same time for Tony and would miss him being around the kitchen. He asked to use her phone so that he could contact Olive and tell her his news and ask if she would get a hold of Mark for him.

Olive was beside herself with joy and said that she would make it happen.

Tony's afternoon was quiet and he stayed close to Liz in the kitchen, just chatting about how his day went and what he had to do before he got to Cornwallis in Nova Scotia.

Supper was meatloaf and Tony ate for two, it was so good. He took a piece of pie up to his room and was settling in for the night when Liz tapped on his door. Olive had called back and said that she had talked to Mark. He would call the next morning and make plans to meet up.

Saturday was a bright, sunny fall morning. Tony had coffee with Mo in the kitchen before he went off to the bar. Near 10:30 AM, Mark did finally phone and said that he would meet Tony that afternoon at a bar just down from the rooming house called "The Lyons". It was an old bar and very small. You had to know it was there because it didn't stick out at all.

Tony already had had two drafts down before Mark came charging through the door, landing at Tony's table with a thump. "You're actually leaving. Ma says you're out of here in seven days?" Tony corrected him, "six days now."

Mark sat down and ordered them a beer and a shot. "Six days" he said, "shit. Tell me about it man." Tony tried to give Mark as much information as he could. He had brought with him his joining instructions, travel orders and schedule.

Mark poured over everything as they drank and talked all afternoon.

In their drunken friendship voices they both said that they would miss each other and a friendship like theirs was forever. Tony had to ask Mark to let go of his hand many times. Finally, Mark said that no matter what, he'd be at the train station to say goodbye.

After hours, they poured out into the street, slapping each other's backs again and again. Tony walked away to his rooming house and Mark went back to the club. When Tony got back to his room he fell right asleep.

Sunday was pretty quiet until people started making noise coming and going in front of the rooming house. He went down to the kitchen and Liz could see he was really hung over. She didn't ask how his meeting with Mark went. Tony said he needed some air, so he grabbed a coffee and went outside in the cool morning and walked along the pier until he started to feel human again.

During the walk he thought of many things, the good, the bad and how a change was in the air. He knew that he had to leave this place and everything there that had marked him. In order to do that he had to see the old man one more time. Tony's new life would not start until he put his past behind him. Wednesday would be an interesting day.

Tony didn't have to worry about the old man not being home. He rarely went anywhere because he usually didn't have money to put gas in his station wagon anyway.

Tony asked Mo if he could use his car on Wednesday afternoon for a few hours and would have it back before Mo had to go to the bar. Mo told Tony he didn't even have to ask, "just take it."

Chapter 37

The week was moving along quicker than Tony wanted, but here he was, one last thing to do. He drove up to the house and parked on the street. He sat in the car for a minute or two before moving. He could see the curtains in the front window moving slightly. He knew he was being watched.

He got out of the car and moved to the front door and knocked. There was no answer, so he banged on the door this time. Still there was no answer. He was getting angry. He knew the old man saw him.

He pushed open the door, and Tony saw the old man and swore that the he hadn't moved or changed since the last time he saw him.

They were at least five feet apart, but Tony could smell the old man's stale sweat and body odor. He didn't get up or look Tony's way, his programs were on. Tony heard him say in a low voice "I hear you're some kind of big bad biker now kid, a real bad-ass. I guess that's something you can be proud of. You look up to them for help and to have your back when you get into shit, and you will, mark my words."

"You mean a father-figure, don't you? Someone that you can be proud of, someone you can look up to? Family should have your back; home should be a safe place to go when you need it. You missed on all those counts, didn't you? It was always the next con."

It went back and forth for a minute or two until Tony became disgusted with the whole thing and told the old man that he had quit the motorcycle club and was moving on.

Tony could see this shocked the old man for a second. "Well," he sneered. "If you're out of the club and not working, what are you going to do with yourself, move back home?" He reached for an old $5 bill from the coffee table and was about to toss it to Tony. "I've got a job you old bastard, I'm leaving Friday."

Tony didn't say another word. He went into his pocket and took out a piece of paper, dropped it on the coffee table and left. Tony drove away and never looked back. Tony envisioned the old man sitting there, looking at the paper on the coffee table. He would sigh deeply and reach for it, and read it. He knew that his mouth would hang open in disbelief. He would be holding a copy of Tony's Oath of Allegiance to the Canadian Forces!

Tony thanked Mo for the loan of the car and went back to his room. He felt a huge weight off his chest and he was feeling calm. There was nothing left for him to do now but leave. He had his bag packed and repacked since Monday, but did it again just to be sure. One last walk on the pier, supper with Liz and Mo and a restful night's sleep brought Friday morning on. It was time to go.

A tearful hug and a bag of sandwiches sent Tony down the road on his way to the train station. It was going to be quite a walk, but the early morning air was cool and fresh. Tony felt good about himself and what was to come.

Chapter 38

The day finally arrived and he was walking to the train station with a determination that was new to him. It was a bright, sun shiny fall day and as he walked he could hear the crunch of the fallen leaves under his feet. Since his focus was getting to the train station, he paid no attention to the traffic or to people walking passed him.

He arrived at the train station, found his departure gate and with a couple of hours to spare he sat on a bench. Tony had never been on a train before and did not know what to expect. The trip would take almost a full day.

Tony started to think about why he was here and what had brought him to this point in his life. He thought about his unbearable childhood, his time with the club, Mark, Betty and finally a chance at a new life.

The sound of a loud speaker clicking on startled Tony from his thoughts. Had he really been there that long already? The unknown voice at the other end of the speaker was announcing the arrival of Via Rail 112 into the station in 15 minutes; it would be changing a few cars, taking on passengers and heading for Montreal and points east. Passengers should be making their way to their assigned platforms to await arrival.

There were many more people now than when he arrived. He was surprised to see that some of the men had sticky nametags on their jackets. Just like the one he had in his folder. Was he supposed to wear it?

The clock was ticking by and he was starting to think that Mark wasn't going to make it.

Just as the speaker announced the arrival of 112, Tony saw the familiar old white Chevy Van screaming into the parking lot.

The train arrived and people were getting off during the short layover to stretch their legs and have a cigarette. Tony was noticing more tags. Mark came running in to the station and out onto the platform, just about crashing into Tony, threw his arms around him and slapped him on the back. "I said I'd be here buddy, there's no way you could get away that easy."

Mark looked like hell in his dirty, worn out jeans that had not been washed in weeks. He wore a pair of old biker boots, his hair tied back with a bandana. Tony was sure he hadn't shaved in days. His dirty biker cut was on full display. It was surprising to Tony, as he realized he had looked somewhat the same only weeks before.

Mark shook Tony's hand again and told him that the club was going out tonight in full force. Because of his arm, he would be driving the van carrying extra weapons and whatever else they needed. Mark was nervously smoking a cigarette and looked like he hadn't slept in a couple of nights.

Tony looked into his eyes, "I'm worried about you man. I can't see anything good coming out of this." He could tell Mark was high on something, but didn't say anything about it. "I'll be fine Tony; Skip said he would look after me." Tony shook his head. Mark looked right at him and said "who is going to have your back buddy, when the bullets start to fly?"

Tony didn't have time to answer. The whistle blew from the station wall. Passengers were starting to board for a five minute departure.

They looked like a pretty odd couple, standing there and shaking each other's hands wildly. As Tony stepped onto the train platform, the train started to pull away and Tony thought he heard Mark yell "good luck!" He then faded into the distance and out of sight.

Tony stood there frozen for a minute then turned to enter the passenger car. He had never been on a train before and he was amazed at how quiet it was inside as it picked up speed and charged down the tracks.

Tony looked into the compartment and found the car was really quite full and a frown came over his face. Finally he noted that down about four rows there were a couple of empty seats, one next to a strange looking guy that Tony thought looked like a hippy. He had long hair, a beat up ball cap, dark John Lennon glasses and a jean jacket and pants that had seen better days.

He looked older than Tony, but what really stood out was that he sported one hell of a large mustache. He was sitting there smoking a cigarette as Tony entered the car and was quietly sizing him up. He caught Tony's eye and motioned to him to take a seat. Tony moved in and sat down next to him.

Tony glanced out of the window one more time, watching as his past moved by. He then focused his attention into the car where he sat with other men just like him. This would be his future.

The guy next to him offered him a smoke, lit it and waited for him to take a drag. The stranger sat back and also took a drag of his cigarette. "I noticed you on the platform" he said with a slight smile, "you hang with some pretty strange dudes there 'pilgrim'". Tony nodded in agreement.

The stranger sat back and put his butt out in the ashtray and looked Tony in the eye. "My name's Keith; you can call me K.G."

BE SURE TO READ THE SEQUEL "CONQUER THE HILL"

From his over-bearing old-man to the street fights and gang wars; Tony has survived Port Nichols and all it had done to try and keep him there. It was time to move on and become the man he was destined to be. He needed to mature, and the military would help him do that and more. Life lessons are sometimes very hard but never boring. Tony will have to face personal peril many times as he decides whether to give in, or clear the shame attached to his name and become a man of honour.

About the Authors!

Warrant Officer, Retired, Larry Edward Crandell, CD Medal; NATO Peacekeeping Medal; Gulf War Medal with Bar; Kuwait Liberation Medal; Order of St John's Medal.

Larry completed 25 years in the Canadian Military, working first on Radar Sites, then for NORAD as an Air Defence Technician. He then worked as a Nuclear Biological Chemical Defence Technician working for NATO in Germany. He is a Veteran of the Gulf War and was there when the night skies lit up as the missiles rained down on Bagdad. Larry spent many nights during the alerts alone in his shelter, out in the desert, writing in his journals about his experiences and wondering what he was doing there. He completed his military career as the Standards Warrant Officer at the Nuclear School in Borden Ontario.

Once retired from the military, he spent a few years working in the Alberta Tar Sands and teaching in Fort McMurray he retired in Saskatoon, Saskatchewan and spends his time writing with his lovely wife of 38 years, Shirley.

Born on the prairies of Saskatchewan, Shirley's career of 35 years was in administration where she took to writing Newsletters and Standing Operating Procedures; and she has always enjoyed writing. She met Larry in 1980 and travelled the world with him and daughter Kathryn. Now retired, she has the time to spend on her personal passions, writing and jewelry making. She has previously published a non-fiction book called "Through the Fog."